SWALLOWED

MEG SMITHERMAN

ROSE & MOTH BOOKS

Editor: Rachel Wharton (Page & Proof)

Cover Design: Adam Wayne

 Created with Vellum

PRAISE FOR SWALLOWED

"A lush, unnerving masterpiece of botanical horror and aching romance. Prepare to be consumed."

Logan Karlie, author of DREAM BY THE SHADOWS

———

"At no point during *Swallowed* did I know what would happen next. Equal parts eerie and visceral, this stunning novella creeps into your bloodstream with merciless precision."

Lindsay Straube, author of KISS OF THE BASILISK

———

"A romantic, propulsive story ... that will stay with you long after the last page."

De Elizabeth, author of THIS RAGING SEA and A SHARED HAUNTING

For everyone who ever looked at a particularly nice tree and thought, "Wait a minute... why he kinda..."

CONTENT WARNINGS

- Mild body horror
- Psychological horror/suspense
- Explicit sex scenes (some involving plants!)
- Discussion/depiction of mental illness

Branches they bore of that enchanted stem,
Laden with flower and fruit, whereof they gave
To each, but whoso did receive of them,
And taste, to him the gushing of the wave
Far far away did seem to mourn and rave
On alien shores; and if his fellow spake,
His voice was thin, as voices from the grave;
And deep-asleep he seem'd, yet all awake,
And music in his ears his beating heart did make.

Alfred, Lord Tennyson
The Lotos-eaters

PROLOGUE

I HAVE DREAMED of the Planet my whole life. It's a recurring heaven that shines brighter than anything on Earth, anything I have ever seen in the waking world. It is verdant slopes of blooms and soft green grass, the widest and bluest sky you could imagine, thick and quiet forests so dark with shadow and moss.

I can't remember a time when the Planet didn't fascinate me. This Earth-like miracle, a blue-green pearl in the deepest reaches of our galaxy. Unthinkably distant, but still within reach.

The Planet is proof that Heaven exists, and we've been there. My mother walked its plains, traversed its forests, and gazed up at its twin moons at dusk. She told me stories all the time — about its beauty, the way it spoke to her heart, how she thinks of it fondly, even now. But she never told me the stories that mattered. Never the ones she told on the news, or in the hearings, or in old interviews for *Time*.

When I was younger, I used to ask her what *really*

happened out there, before I was born. Was she a hero who survived a cursed mission? A villain, doomed by popular narrative? But no matter what I asked, she would only frown and turn away. When I remember it now, it's like she was afraid I'd see the truth in her eyes, whatever that was.

Eventually, I learned to stop asking her.

I've seen all the interviews; I've read all the articles. Some of them paint her as the lucky sole survivor. Some of them are damning. But they all ask the question: Why did only she make it back when the rest were left for dead? And she never truly answered. Maybe she didn't know. Maybe she was just as confused as everyone else.

When my mother finally died, the end of a slow creep toward eternity that seemed so wrong for someone still so young, I said goodbye to a woman I had never known.

But I know the Planet. I've seen it in my dreams.

"JILL."

My name jolts me out of distraction. Reluctant, I turn away from the tiny porthole window. I don't want to stop looking at the Planet's lengthening curve, growing closer with every second. I blow out an impatient breath. "What?"

Darcie scowls good-naturedly. "Stop hogging the window." She leans over me awkwardly, still strapped in tight as we grow close to breaking atmo, her thick black hair tickling my nose.

"Should've paid for the window seat," I say, trying to flatten myself backward, giving Darcie more room. "This is basic stuff. Mensa member my ass."

She shoots me a withering side-eye. "You know, Jill—"

"She's right, though," Julian adds from the other side of the cramped shuttle, framed by the starlit shape of their porthole. "Premium seats for free? In *this* economy?"

"Exactly," I say, my mouth practically inside Darcie's

ear the way she's craning into my space. "I thought you were smart."

"Apparently not smart enough to get out of a mission peopled by incompetents," she says pleasantly, still peering eagerly out the porthole. Then, cheerfully under her breath, "J names are always such dick—"

"Okay, that's enough," Ben interrupts from beside Julian. His presence is suddenly imposing, as if he can turn his leadership off and on like a switch. Probably comes with being military. Unlike us scientists, our brains running a million miles a minute, always joking and fucking around to let off steam, he's a landmine. He waits patiently. And then, when the team gets rowdy, or there's a problem that needs solving, he snaps into action. And he's suddenly *there*, undeniable, and I can't look away.

"Sorry, Dad," Julian singsongs.

Ben pinches his nose with blunt fingers. "Fleming, how many times do I have to say it? Do not call me *Dad*."

"Yes, Dad," Darcie says.

I refuse to join in on the joke. It feels too comfortable, especially around Ben. In the year the four of us have been training together, I still haven't let him in. Darcie and Julian are my friends now, for better or worse. But something about Ben makes me feel unsteady, and it's easier to hold him at arm's length than look my own feelings in the eye. I tell the others it's the fact he's military, but that's only part of it.

Ben shoots me a look as if to say, *Save me from them*, and I shrug, turning away.

Darcie and Julian begin bickering across the shuttle, and their voices fade to the background as my attention turns back to the porthole. The Planet rises toward us. I am already in love. I've seen her before in tapes and photographs. I've seen her rivers, mountains, and woods. Her deserts and weather patterns. But not like this. Not from space, approaching her from outside. She is an egg, ready to hatch. And we're her fertilizer.

I see humanity as it will be if our mission succeeds, making a new home on the Planet: First, a few thousand colonists, then doubling, then quadrupling, building, and spreading. Diverting rivers and carving through mountains. Thriving in our new home. My chest aches.

The background hum of jovial bickering grows loud and harsh.

"Don't be such a killjoy," says Darcie, "we're not even there yet."

"I'm not being a *killjoy*," Julian retorts, pushing a pair of oval glasses up their long nose. "God forbid I speculate on the philosophical nature of this mission."

"You weren't speculating, you dweeb," Darcie says, facing away from me. "You were being crass. *Cursed?* Really? Bitch, we're scientists."

"Science can't explain everything, bitch."

Ben sighs, running a hand down his face. He's older than the three of us, though not by much. I've never asked, but I'd guess he's in his late thirties, maybe forty. He has the long-suffering air of a man who's used to putting up with bullshit. Another side effect of years in the armed forces.

"It can, and it does," Darcie almost shouts across the too-small shuttle. "What conspiracy sites have you been frequenting? Are you a flat-earther now?"

"Nobody's a flat-earther, Farreira," Ben rumbles. His voice is rough, low, and gravelly, made for giving orders.

"What if I am" Julian says defiantly.

"Immediate ejection from the shuttle," declares Darcie.

"You would *kill* me for having an unorthodox way of thinking?"

"Jesus, Jules, I swear—"

"What are you assholes arguing about?" I cut in. But I think I already know. It's the same thing they've been whispering about for the past year, ever since the four of us got placed together on this team, ever since I told them who my mom was.

An awkward silence falls over the shuttle.

"Ignore them, Jones," Ben says. He always calls us by our last names.

"Julian's being a dillweed," Darcie says at the same time.

"If you didn't want to be on this mission, Jules," I say, crossing my arms and leveling a ripe glare across the shuttle, "you should have thought of that three months ago before you crawled into your hyper-sleep pod." I hate that it bothers me, the stuff people say about my mother and what happened to her on this planet. Good or bad, it has nothing to do with me. But sometimes, when it's quiet and I allow my mind to go there, I believe the bad things: the imagined darkness my mother endured at the end of a mission that fell apart.

"Like I'd turn it down," Julian says haughtily. "Life-changing opportunity."

I snort but say nothing else. They won't meet my gaze; they know they've crossed a line.

Darcie turns to me, her expression pained. "I'm sorry. I shouldn't have let them bait me. It's just... I'm sure you're a little on edge, right? No one ever found out exactly what—"

"No, I know," I interrupt. This is the first time anyone has brought it up since I told them about my mom. I guess the anticipation and anxiety has finally made it impossible to keep their mouths shut. Not that I blame them, really. "They never found the bodies," I finish for Darcie. "But I'm sure... I'm sure it was nothing crazy. She was scared, on an alien planet, watching her team drop like flies. No one would want to relive that. Or maybe she just forgot most of it. The trauma and everything."

Darcie eyes me. "You mean she never even told *you*—"

"And that's enough of that, kids," Ben cuts in with finality. "This isn't a ghost-hunting trip. This is a reconnaissance mission for the ECE. Testing the Planet for viability. Got it? No one is to get carried away discussing missing *bodies*."

"Yes, sir," Darcie says, dripping sarcasm.

"Ben," he says, leaning his head back against his seat and closing his eyes. "It's Ben. None of you people are in the military, and 'sir' makes me sound like your dom."

"Sorry, sir," Julian says, grinning.

We all recede into silence as we break atmo. Heat and light rush past us, but within the lightly vibrating shuttle, we're in the eye of the storm. I can't help but grip my seat, fingers taut, as I stare out the porthole.

And then in a flash, we're through, we're *here*, within the Planet's embrace.

She rises up to greet us, inescapable in her glory. A blue sea expands like a white-flecked jewel below us, wide and glimmering in the morning light. As we descend, tiny islands materialize, emerald green and untouched. Soon, the greater continent looms below, and I know that we're perfectly on course. I never doubted the shuttle's auto-pilot navigation, but a little tension fades from my shoulders anyway. And then there are mountains within view, snow-capped and violent in their suddenness, lit up by the cresting sun. Watching her take shape below us, I'm eager. Despite what Julian said, I'm not afraid of what's already happened. I trust the Planet. I'm ready to plant my feet on her shores.

After all, this might be our new home.

"Hang on tight," Ben announces, his voice cutting through my abstraction.

"The landing is supposed to be gentle," Julian gripes.

"It *will* be gentle," Ben says. "But just in case, hang on."

"To what?" Darcie asks.

"Your hats," Ben suggests.

Eager anticipation buzzes in the air. We're all smiling, the tension from before gone entirely. Darcie's trying to get a good look through the porthole again, pushing into my personal space.

"I'm not wearing a hat," says Julian.

We're close now.

The ground flies up to meet us. With a swoop in my gut, I realize I recognize this forest. I've seen these thickening trees, and I recognize this plain, the meandering river and its crescent-bright oxbow lakes. I've seen them in tapes, training materials, pamphlets, and posters, of course. But most vividly, I've seen them in my dreams.

A tang of fear slides up from my gut and into my

mouth. What if the landing *isn't* gentle? We've never done this before. None of us are pilots; that's why the navigation is automatic. What happens if the shuttle goes off course? If it lands wrong? What if — there are so many things that could go wrong. My mother was here before, and everything went wrong. Everything. What if that's our fate, too?

Individual blades of grass scream up to meet us. Flowers wave in the backdraft.

"Brace for landing," says Ben.

"Fuck, fuck, fuck," Julian chants.

Suddenly, the shuttle is stationary, then it swings backward and upward. Unearthed clods of grass whip past the portholes, dirt churning up around us. We descend again, slowly, the shuttle's engines stirring up earth and plant matter.

And with a soft jolt, so gentle it's almost imperceptible, we land.

"WELP," says Ben, unstrapping himself and standing. "We made it, gang. Let's get this show on the road."

No one says anything.

"You good?" Ben says, fixing each of us with a look of impatient concern.

Am I good? I find there are words trapped in my throat, but I can't voice them. We made it. We're on a new planet, light-years from Earth, and we're supposed to take off our seatbelts and just get up and carry on? In a second, alien air will be touching my face. Alien grass will tickle my ankles. We'll be only the second team of humans to come here. Ever.

Reality sinks in slowly.

"Kids, get your shit together," Ben says, and at least his tone is gentle. "I said, you good?"

"Good," says Julian, their voice faint. I glance over and see that their face has gone sickly pale.

"Good," murmurs Darcie. She meets my gaze, her eyes shining with tears.

"I'm good," I echo. I grab Darcie's hands and squeeze them. We grin maniacally, shaking our hands together. *We're here*, the action seems to say. *We fucking made it.*

"Good," grunts Ben. He grins, too. "Let's get the hell out there."

Before we gather our gear, we all head outside to take in the Planet. To really absorb the fact that we're living the dream we've had for years, the mission we gave up a year of our life training for. As we clamber after Ben into the morning light, I'm overwhelmed by a cascade of awe. I think all of us are.

No one says much beyond a soft "*Wow,*" or "*Fuck,*" murmuring quiet feelings aloud, each of us in a moment of solitude, of private wonder.

The plain stretches out on all sides, silver-green. The grass is tall, almost waist height for me and Julian, a bit lower on Darcie and Ben, and waving like a verdant sea. I want to hold it, study it, and understand how it works. Does the grass require photosynthesis, like Earth flora? My mother's mission was never able to collect all the information it needed, beyond the basics. I can't wait to know every flower here, every tree, every seedling. There is so much here to learn and cherish, it's almost too much for me to contemplate.

While the other two wander in small circles, staring out at this wide new world, I notice Ben with a tinge of irritation at myself. I need to stop *noticing* him. He's already snapped into leader mode, consulting his tablet, turning various dials, and adjusting its antenna. He peers out over the waving plain, its curves and dips, the black shadow of a forest in the distance, eyes narrowed. Does he see the beauty we do? Does he care?

Apparently reaching some unspoken deadline, Ben snaps his fingers. "All right, time to move. We landed a bit off course. It's a three-hour hike to the camp instead of one."

Darcie makes a face. "We just landed on an alien planet. Can't we, I don't know, take a second?"

Ben crosses his arms. "For what? You wanna write some poetry?"

"Surprised you know what that is," Julian says. The wind picks up, buffeting their usually pristine curtains of black hair across their face.

"I contain multitudes."

Julian gives Ben a slow once-over. "Your eye to bicep ratio says otherwise."

Darcie turns to stare at Julian. "His what?"

"My *what*?"

"He has small eyes and huge biceps. The mark of a meathead."

I snort a laugh.

"No..." Darcie says, peering at Ben's tall and fit body, short brown hair, broad shoulders, and trim waist. She tilts her head to one side. "No, I get it."

Ben sighs, staring up at the sky. "Jesus Christ."

"Also," Julian adds, eyeing Ben's sidearm, "the gun removes like, fifty points from intellect."

"Right, okay, you've had your second," Ben says. "Five minutes to load up your gear, and then we're out."

We're all excited chatter as we heft our packs from the shuttle's storage compartment, zip up our standard-issue utility jackets, and switch on our walkie-talkies. We'll be heading east, and the sun is vivid and sharp, unobscured by clouds. When we're all ready, spirits high, Ben lifts an arm to indicate we're moving out.

He cuts a line through the undulating plain, his green cargoes and jacket almost gray against the Planet's saturated colors. A steady wind flows eastward as if it means to help guide us. The tall grasses lean forward, eager and supplicant. Here and there, clusters of flowers splash the green like scattered paint from a brush, unexpected and vibrant.

The ground is easy to traverse. No hidden pebbles or stones push up from the soil to trip us. There are no animal burrows underfoot, ready to roll an unsuspecting ankle. The Planet, based on my mother's limited information and the data sent back by probes, plays host to very few animals. There are no predators that might be a danger to us. Not even venomous snakes or poisonous frogs in the rain-drenched forests. Only a strange breed of deer, very shy; a rabbit-like mammal, seemingly nocturnal; and the birds, which keep to the skies and themselves, never seeking out human company. Why would they? We're utterly strange to them.

Darcie and I walk side by side. Julian trails behind. Ben is far ahead of us now, but we make no attempt to hurry. It's morning, and we'll reach the camp well before sunset. There has never been a major weather event on this part of the continent; not since the ECE started monitoring it as a potential colony site.

It's perfectly safe.

But we all know what happened last time. My mother

came here with seven others, and one by one, they disappeared. All but my mother.

A relentless dread surfaces inside me, and I try to tamp it down. Because this place... I breathe her in, her clean air, and I feel the rustle of grass against my legs, and my chest fills with the most overwhelming sense of *right*. Whatever happens, we belong here. This planet is too perfect to pass up. As if she was made just for us.

"Look," Darcie breathes. Her hand is outstretched, fingers drifting over the tops of bending grass. As she drags her fingers over the blades, they follow her. And for a few moments, the grass that touches her skin leans inward, turning perpendicular to the flow of the wind. It holds, motionless, reaching for her.

It takes me a minute to understand what I'm seeing. "Mimosa pudica," I murmur.

"What?" Darcie says, turning.

"Mimosa pudica," Julian echoes, joining us. "Duh. Does anyone else feel weird, though?"

"No," says Darcie. "Why?"

"Weird how?" I ask.

Julian shrugs, frowning. "Like unsettled. I dunno." They look out toward the horizon. "Doesn't it feel different from Earth? Too quiet. Too pretty."

"No way," Darcie says. "Prettier and quieter than *Earth*? The war-torn, over-populated hunk of rock with more hurricanes and droughts than naturally occurring trees? How fucking strange."

"I'm trying to be honest about my feelings in the moment," Julian says, raising their chin. "Guess *someone* didn't take their psych training course seriously."

Darcie rolls her eyes.

"I get what you mean," I say, catching Julian's eye. "Maybe it's how Earth used to be, but it doesn't feel real."

"Exactly, thank you, *Jill*," Julian says pointedly while glaring at Darcie.

She rolls her eyes again. "You need to start making use of your standard-issue drug supply, Jules. Maybe a tranquilizer to shut you up."

"Then you'd have to carry me to camp. Good idea."

"No, I'd leave you here to rot."

"Enjoy the beating from Ben."

"Maybe I *will*."

The good-natured bickering goes on, but I'm no longer listening. I'm running my fingers gently along each blade of grass. If I touch them one at a time, they sort of shiver. And then, as I crouch to run my finger up one stem to the tip, it curves toward me as if chasing the sensation. Reaching for me. Wanting me.

I can't drag my eyes away. I can't stop. The grass is beautiful. Each blade is emerald green on one side, velvety silver on the other, and soft-edged. Gentle. A vibrating excitement builds in my chest. An aching joy. I've never seen anything so—

"Jill, what the fuck are you doing down there?" Julian asks.

I glance up, squinting. "Like I said, Mimosa pudica. It must be the same evolutionary mechanism."

Darcie joins Julian to stand over me curiously. "Speak English, plant nerd."

I stand, brushing off my hands on my thighs. "You know those ferns," I begin, stretching out a finger and then curling it inward, "the ones that do that when you touch them?"

"Yeah," Darcie says.

Julian blinks. "Mimosa pudica, I know."

"Well, Darcie doesn't," I say. "The grass. Touch it, watch."

We all stretch out our hands. As our skin brushes the bending grass, it responds. We create three small gravity wells, pulling grasses inward as we spin slowly, running our palms over the foliage. It's the strangest, most bizarre feeling in the world. Natural greenery, so much of it, a *sea* of it. And not only are we here among it, touching it, experiencing it, but it's experiencing us *back*.

Darcie's walkie-talkie crackles. *Gang, come in.*

Darcie presses on the walkie with her thumb. "Yeah?"

I stop spinning and stare eastward, at Ben's small figure in a waving sea of green. He raises one arm.

Stop playing around, and move your asses.

We all laugh. I feel euphoric. Sick with excitement. This is only the start.

"Sorry, sir," Darcie says into the walkie. "Coming."

The grass caresses us the whole way to the base camp. Every once in a while, one of us puts out a hand to let it brush our skin. We pass through a spray of magenta flowers. None of us touches a petal, but the blooms face us as we pass and seem to watch us as we travel east.

I SIGNED up for the expedition because I believe in second chances. I wanted to see the Planet, yes; maybe even to follow in my mother's footsteps in some twisted way. But it wasn't just that. It was the dream of a new home for humanity. We killed Earth. Millions of us died, wiped out in horrific weather events, from starvation, or from exposure in the massive deserts that bloomed in the Great Heating Event. And worse, we killed each other, ravaged the land with bombs, no longer concerned with preserving humanity, let alone the environment. There was nothing left to save.

Then we received a transmission from one of our far-reaching probes, one of our last hopes for the future. And there she was, only a few light-years away: the Planet, as if handed to us by God himself, to cleanse us of our sins.

At first, they sent more probes, with ways to measure the atmosphere, water content, biology, everything that might impact our ability to settle there. Probe after probe went out to the Planet, and one by one they sent back data, millions of terabytes of data, all reaching one conclusion:

The Planet will be humanity's salvation.

A year later, the first manned mission departed for the Planet, my mother among them.

She was the only one who came back.

If Earth wasn't so ruined, if there was any evidence at all that the Planet was inherently perilous, the Earth Colonization Effort might have put a stop to all manned missions going forward. But they didn't.

Instead, they took a few decades to send more probes. They got more scientists involved, including me. And finally, when everything was determined to be utterly safe, they opened recruitment for the second manned mission to the Planet.

I have never believed in anything so fervently as I believe in the ECE. Whether it's my mother's blood, my obsession with the green and growing, or hard-wired optimism — the Planet is everything to me. It is hope incarnate. And no matter what happened to my mother's team, no matter what unknown horrors might have befallen them, I have to believe it won't happen again.

This place is too good, too right. I know in the marrow of my bones that this is where we're meant to be.

I believe it so strongly; I'm drowning in it.

BASE CAMP IS a cluster of tents against a hill, nestled in a dirt clearing at the edges of the forest. It was left here by my mother's expedition; everything as it was, down to the lab tents and all their equipment. It's been here for thirty-two years, and everything is intact. The camp is clean, organized. Like it's sat here in stasis for decades, waiting.

A wide, shallow river meanders to the north of camp, which we already know is safe to drink and perfect for bathing.

Darcie, Julian, and I each claim a tent, side by side on the southern side of camp. The tents are barely tall enough to stand up in. Each is fitted with a cot, a hook for our lanterns, and a storage trunk. I'm strangely disappointed to find that mine has nothing interesting inside. A few socks, their owner unidentifiable. A blanket, some random tools, and a length of rope. What did I expect, a note from my mother?

It feels wrong, somehow, to be taking up residence

where seven people used to live; six who never had a chance to say goodbye.

Ben chooses a tent on the north side of the camp. The centrally located main tent is spacious and outfitted with a long table, a massive freezer stocked with rotten food, and impersonal necessities. Everything else, we brought on our backs. I packed light, not planning to do much outside of work, but I know Darcie has a veritable library inside her pack. Julian brought sketchbooks, paints, and charcoal. None of us know what Ben brought.

"Probably porn mags, protein jerky, and guns," Julian muses, joining me on the way to the main tent.

It's evening, and Darcie has been cooking for the past hour. She and Ben managed to get the generator up and running, and Darcie, to her glee and everyone else's dismay, found a stock of canned goods with no expiration date. She'd said it was a celebration, and since she's the only one of us who can make a decent meal, she took it upon herself to cook.

"Guns plural?" I ask.

"He's packing untold amounts of heat, I just know it," Julian says. Their favorite hobby is razzing Ben, regardless of whether or not he's present. "Guns hidden in every nook and crevice. Bet there's one up his ass."

"Something's up his ass, gun or not."

Julian guffaws. "Why do they send military on these missions anyway?"

"Because you're an idiot." Ben comes around the other side of the main tent, hands in his pockets. "Someone's gotta keep an eye on you."

"Oh no," Julian says dramatically. "You heard that? I didn't mean it, Papa."

"You know, I *can* go back to the shuttle," says Ben. "Back to Earth. Leave you three here to conduct your little tests all alone. But when something comes for you in the night..." he draws a finger across his throat, and his eyes are shining with an unspent smile.

Julian snorts, ducking into the main tent as Ben holds the flap door open for us. "What's gonna come for me in the night," they say, "a bunny rabbit?"

"Those are actually rodents," Darcie snipes over her shoulder from where she's finishing up dinner. There are steaming pots on the stove and several opened cans on a table nearby with labels like *Dehydrated Cheese Product* and *Essence of Carrot*. "The rabbits here," she continues when no one immediately responds. "They're not rabbits."

"No shit," says Julian.

"Rabbits are rodents," Ben says with complete confidence, going over to Darcie and offering a hand. She shoves him away.

"They're not," all three scientists chime as one.

Ben frowns and settles himself at one of the long tables, giving up on trying to help Darcie. Julian is already seated and waiting. We both know Darcie better than to try to interfere with her projects.

"But their teeth," Ben says, leaning forward on his elbows and catching my eye. "They have the... you know. Rodent teeth."

"*The* rodent teeth?" I bite back a laugh, unable to hold his gaze.

"They're big in the front," he clarifies, tapping one of his incisors.

"It's like interacting with a toddler," says Darcie.

Julian turns to Ben. "You stick to your myriad guns, and we'll handle the rodents."

"I have one gun."

"So you say."

I settle myself at the table next to Julian, across from Ben. "Darce," I venture, "did you find the wine store?" It's in all my mother's interviews. Her expedition brought copious amounts of wine, one thing we were forbidden to do — no alcohol, no mind-altering drugs, no sex paraphernalia. But no one can prevent us from partaking in what's already here.

Darcie scoffs. "Who do you think I am? *Did I find the wine store.*" She hefts a crate and slams it on the table. "Voila. Only the finest for humanity's last hope."

Julian makes a sound of disbelief, standing to open the crate. They pull out a bottle. "No," they breathe.

I lean across the table and grab a bottle of my own, reading the label. I read it again. "Is this real?"

Ben yanks the bottle out of my hand, peering at the label, his brows drawn. "No way."

"Yes way," Darcie says brightly.

"Grape wine," I breathe, stealing the bottle back from Ben. Our fingers brush for a fraction of a second. I swallow, distracted by the warm roughness of his fingers.

"Well?" Julian demands, waving a hand at me. "Read us the label, Queen Botanica."

I clear my throat. "Chateau Pacifico, Genuine Terra Reserve. Red House Blend."

"I've heard of this," Ben declares proudly, like he's always wanted to be the guy who recognizes a type of grape. It's annoyingly charming. "The Napa greenhouses used to grow them. Grapes aren't as good as they used to be, but they're real, grown in the soil. No chemicals."

"Not as *many* chemicals," Darcie corrects, setting a steaming pot in the center of the table. "Eat up, babes. I call it Heroes of Humanity Stew. Why isn't the wine open?"

"We're studying it," I say.

"It's an archaeological discovery," Julian adds. "I mean, this is *old* and *expensive*."

"What's in the stew?" Ben asks, eyeing the pot.

Darcie shrugs, producing a ladle and holding it out to him. "Bit of everything, plus some secret ingredients."

"Is the secret ingredient Dehydrated Cheese Product?" Julian asks warily.

Darcie smiles. "I shall neither confirm nor deny. Listen, there's protein in it. And what passes as vegetables. It's *nutritious*. Eat."

"Better than space food," says Ben, and he begins serving us heaping bowls of stew.

I open the wine. It's vacuum sealed, and the second I break the seal, I inhale the wine's earthy, rich scent. I could really use a drink. I'm starting to feel fatigued, or maybe dehydrated — like everything's too much and too real, all at once. I'm here. We're *here*, but somehow it feels like I'm still in one of my dreams.

"Jones," Ben says, "you gonna keep that wine for yourself?"

"Sorry," I say, realizing I should be celebrating along with everyone else. I pour four cups and pass them around.

"A toast?" Darcie suggests, holding hers aloft.

"To this fucking weird planet," Julian declares.

Darcie rolls her eyes. Ben side-eyes Julian.

"To the Planet," I say, and I mean it.

"The Planet," everyone echoes.

The wine tastes like loam and nutmeg and what I can only assume is grape. It's completely different from any wine I've tasted before. It's richer, more complex, but somehow cleaner. It's been taken from the bosom of Earth herself. We're drinking to our new home with the blood of our old.

We drain our cups, and Julian opens the next bottle, filling them again with ruby liquid. After a few days of subsisting on dehydrated space food, the stew is heavenly despite its questionable content. Everything begins to feel warm and hazy, soft-edged. I can't stop looking at Ben's hands.

"Listen," Julian announces after a while, their wine sloshing as they raise the cup aloft. We've all consumed at least a bottle each — the stores are expansive. "Benjamin."

"Please, not Benjamin," Ben mutters, lowering his forehead to his arms, folded on the table in front of him.

"*Benjamin*. Papa Benjamin. I want to discuss the guns. And why you have them, but we don't."

"Shut the fuck up," Darcie drawls, every word spoken with obvious love. Her eyes shine in the orange light. The sun has set, and outside, a chorus of crickets wavers in and out of hearing. But they can't be crickets. Crickets only exist on Earth. As far as we know, there are no insects on the Planet. These are something else, some other sound. Birds? Bats? Frogs?

"None of you need a gun," says Ben.

"What if I do, though?" Julian insists, leaning into Ben. "It's a power imbalance. What if you go insane?"

Darcie and I shoot each other a look to say *not this again*. Julian's imagination and tendency to chafe under authority have always been a source of annoyance and entertainment for the team. But I had hoped maybe they'd mellow out once we got to the Planet.

"I'll take it under advisement," Ben says, sitting up and leaning back in his chair. He's unbuttoned the top few buttons of his jacket, revealing a white fitted Henley underneath.

"I'm *serious*," Julian insists.

"So am I," Ben says. "If you're good, maybe I'll let you hold my gun. Now, that's enough talk of deadly weapons. Tonight's a celebration."

5

THE AIR in the tent is warm and close. I take a long drink of wine, relishing the way it rolls thickly down my throat. I lick my lips.

Ben's gaze falls on me for a breath. For a second, I wonder if he can tell what I'm thinking. Can he tell how hard I try not to look at him, touch him, laugh with him? He must think I hate him.

I become vaguely aware of the fact that I'm drunk.

Darcie and Julian are laughing about some shared joke, clasping hands across the table, tears streaming down their faces. A half-eaten sleeve of freeze-dried cookies Darcie fished out of the food store sits next to the wine. One of the cookies has fallen out onto the table and is soaking up a bit of spilled wine. The stew has long since gone cold.

Ben keeps looking at me, like he's trying to get my attention.

My breath catches. The night creeps in and leans over me, fingers my throat. There is so much to see and touch, so many strands of life to follow, beating hearts and growing things. And Ben is distracting the fuck out of me. I need fresh air.

I push back my chair and stand abruptly. No one seems to notice. The floor tilts as I walk; I've had way too much to drink. I push open the tent flap, and the night greets me.

I take a long, deep breath of night air and gaze up at the sky. I have never seen anything like it, except in photographs. They don't begin to do it justice. The sky is so clear that I believe, for a moment, I could fly. That all I'd need to do is push off gently, and up and up I'd float, called to the star-flecked night.

It's not at all like looking out at space from a porthole window. It's richer, more vivid, better. The stars curve over us like a net of fireflies, and *there*, faintly glowing, a drift of star-snow, is the Milky Way Galaxy. So far from home, each star unfamiliar, and yet we share this. In this moment, I know that we are all connected, from the worms in the dirt to the beacon-bright stars at the farthest edge of the galaxy.

I could stand here forever until I starve to death and collapse into nothing. I could do it happily.

"Jones, you okay?"

The warm hand on my shoulder doesn't startle me, but my heart speeds anyway.

I turn, and there stands Ben. His jaw is darkening with five-o'clock shadow. His eyes are bright with wine. He drops his hand as if realizing belatedly it was too familiar. "Bit too much to drink?"

I nod stiffly.

"Me too."

His presence irritates me. I was having a moment,

taking in the beauty. And now he's here, this unavoidable man, smelling faintly of sweat and wine. Doesn't he know I can't think of anything else when he's this close to me? I wish he'd go away. But he just stands there, looking up at the stars.

"You know," he says, "my buddies back home would never let me live this down."

Back home. We've been away for months, in hypersleep for most of that time. And before that, we were training in a top secret base with zero outside contact. I hardly know what home is anymore.

"Live what down?"

I feel his gaze on me, but I keep my eyes on the sky. "Stargazing," he says, then shakes his head. "Getting *emotional* while stargazing."

"Are you getting emotional?"

"Impossible not to."

Interesting. "I think your buddies would get it."

"You don't know my buddies."

"It's the *stars*."

He huffs a breath, and it turns to condensation in the cold night air. "Maybe they'd get it if I was getting choked up over a new model of unmanned precision strike drone."

I can't help but laugh at that.

He smiles. "Nah, it's not just the stars. This place... the Planet. I don't know how to describe it, but—"

A soft alarm begins to chime. Ben frowns, checks his watch, then presses a button to turn off the alarm. "Anomaly on the sensors."

"What is it?"

"Hard to say. Some kind of faint energy burst. It's flickering in and out. I won't be able to do a full read on the equipment until I can get our tech tent up and running."

"Can't you track it with your watch?"

He glances at me, searching. "Yeah. Maybe. When it's daylight."

"Right."

"Jones?"

I stiffen. "Yeah?"

"Why did you come here?"

God, I've had too much wine for this conversation. Or maybe, I've had exactly the right amount. If I was sober, I'd ditch him right now. As it is, I can barely meet his gaze, so I look back up at the sky. "I had no other choice," I say, surprised at myself for the honesty. Usually, I answer that it's the scientist in me, an ingrained desire for progress, something palatable and good for sound bites.

"Which means?"

I grit my teeth. Why won't he leave me alone? He disturbed my stargazing, and now he's asking probing questions. "It's just that my entire life has revolved around this planet," I admit, shrugging like it's nothing when, in fact, it's everything. "I grew up in the public eye with a famous botanist mom who happened to survive a horrific and extremely publicized incident. It was kind of impossible to avoid. And unfortunately for me, I inherited the science gene."

In my periphery, I see Ben smile crookedly. "I remember seeing you on TV."

My cheeks flush hot. Oh, God. "No, you don't."

"I do. You'd just published a paper on the Planet's ecosystem or something, and every science network had you pegged as the next big thing in biology. They kept saying people like you would change the world."

"That's fucking embarrassing," I mutter, praying he can't see how red I am in the twin moonlight. I remember the interview he's referencing. I was on CNN discussing the Planet, arguing in favor of a new expedition. I didn't just sign up for this mission, and Ben knows it. I made sure it happened.

"Why?" he asks.

I turn, and his expression is soft, genuine. *Fucking irritating*. "I sounded like such a pretentious dick," I admit. "And the glasses I was wearing? I don't even need a prescription. I thought they made me look intelligent. I'm so sorry you had to witness that."

He smirks. "I'm not."

"Well, I've improved as a person since then."

"I thought you were great."

"Oh," I say, caught off guard by the night and the wine and, as always, Ben. "Okay. Well. Thanks."

He stretches, arms above his head. His t-shirt lifts, and a sliver of skin appears above his cargo pants.

I quickly look away. "I should go to bed."

Ben sighs, dropping his arms. "Me too. 'Night, Jones."

When I get back to my tent, I change into my pajamas. I wash my face with a cleansing pad and brush my teeth. Laughter and voices cut comfortingly through the silence as Darcie and Julian head to bed, as we all get ready to spend our first night on the Planet.

I lie awake for what feels like an eternity, listening to the wind and the cricket-like sounds. I wonder if Darcie and Julian will go to bed together. They're both young, attractive. We're all young, I guess. I don't think of myself as attractive — my chin-length hair is too muddy to be considered brunette, my eyes aren't much better, and I probably have too many freckles — but Ben is.

I squirm in my cot. Thank God I didn't help myself to more wine at dinner, or I might have made a complete fool of myself out there with Ben. Whatever this is, this ridiculous crush of mine, it needs to die. It was bad enough in training, but everything on the Planet feels heightened. Sharper, hungrier. And I *am* hungry.

Rolling over and pressing my hot face into my pillow, I listen for the telltale sounds of the others hooking up. Breathy moans, giggles in the quiet. But there's nothing.

I think of Ben, gazing up at the stars. Our fingers brushing, his hand on my shoulder. The fact that he *liked* those stupid glasses. "Fuck," I mumble into the pillow. He's annoying. A jock. Not my type at *all*, and kind of my boss. I need to get my shit together.

I toss and turn for what feels like hours, unable to sleep. The night is wide and wanting, and so am I. It's been so long since I let myself *feel*.

Sighing in surrender, I roll onto my back. I run a hand from my breasts to my stomach, feather-light. I'm achingly alone in this cot, in the dark. The night agrees, and the sky comes down to join me, to cradle me in its soft blackness. In a half-asleep haze, I work myself to a breathless ache, needy for release. Only when I'm desperate, ready to cry out for my own touch, do I press a thumb to my tender core. Only then do I curl my fingers inside, stroking the tight, wet center of myself, my eyes shut tight against the world.

The Planet blooms around me. Sprouts break through

the tent floor, curling up and opening, erupting in color as I cover my mouth with my hand to muffle my ecstatic cry. The stars are careening into me, and I'm opening up for them, my orgasm expanding and contracting like the womb of the earth.

I sleep well after that, and when I wake, I remember no dreams.

6

I JOLT awake to the sound of gunshots. My pulse skyrockets, my skin heats, and the hairs on my neck prickle as adrenaline shoots through me. Something's gone wrong.

I trip over myself as I scramble to get dressed, pulling on my cargo pants and wrenching a black t-shirt over my head. I don't even lace my boots before dashing out of my tent toward the *pop-pop* of discharged firearms. I have a horrible vision of Darcie losing her mind in the fashion of a horror film, stealing Ben's gun, and going on a rampage through camp.

I'm just sprinting past the main tent when I hear laughter. Darcie's laughter is open and generous, more like a guffaw than anything. Then Julian's irritable voice and Ben's low rumble. I slow to a walk, my chest heaving.

Christ almighty.

"You assholes nearly gave me a heart attack!" I call out, rounding the main tent to see them all gathered at the edge of the plain.

The three assholes turn as one, and Darcie waves, smiling brightly. "Rise and shine!" she shouts.

"It's literally..." I check my watch, turning a dial to the time setting, "Six-thirty in the morning. Why are we playing with guns?"

"I blackmailed Ben into teaching me how to shoot," Julian announces from where they're crouched on trampled grass, their elbows braced on a crate, a gun in their hands. Ben crouches next to them in just his cargoes and t-shirt, one hand braced on the crate, silver dog tag chain winking against the back of his tan neck. The other hand holds a mug of coffee.

"You slept too late," Darcie says, sipping from her own mug. "We figured this was just as good as an alarm."

"An alarm that takes five years from your life," I mutter. I give her a sidelong glance. "You're not bothered by this?"

"By what?" She raises her eyebrows, daring me to elaborate.

I shrug. I won't say anything in front of Ben. He never connected with Darcie and Julian like I did, never stayed up until the small hours of the morning sharing baggage like it was show-and-tell. Darcie doesn't like to talk about her ex, what he did to her, or what she did to him when it all got to be too much — I'm surprised she's okay being this close to an active gun.

"What you need is caffeine," Darcie says, turning away. "I'm assuming you slept badly?"

"I didn't sleep at *all*," Julian declares like it's a bragging right. "In fact, I should submit a complaint against Benjamin for letting me handle a live weapon in such a state."

Ben takes a long-suffering drag of coffee.

"I see you've changed your tune," I say, moving closer to Darcie and wiggling my fingers. She hands me her coffee, and I take a long swig. "Suddenly pro-gun now, are we?"

"Oh, yes," Julian says, all focus as they line up their aim. "I've already set up a monthly donation to the Earth Rifle Association."

"Gentle," Ben says, all his focus on Julian. "Let your hands drift. Both eyes open."

"I *know*," Julian grumbles.

"You're too stiff," says Ben. "Squeeze the trigger slow. Gentle. No sudden movements."

"This is fascinating," Darcie breathes, yanking her coffee out of my grasp. "Julian, suddenly addicted to guns? Who would have thought."

"It's for protection," Julian snaps.

"Against?" Darcie asks.

"The Man."

"Which man?"

"Me, obviously," Ben says, distracted. "No, no, don't—"

Pop!

Julian fires the gun, and their hands fly back, almost hitting their chin.

"We'll work on controlling the recoil," says Ben with a sigh. "And what did I say about *gentle*?"

"Yeah yeah, Dad," Julian says.

"What are you aiming at?" I ask. I've been trying to figure it out. They seem to be firing into the empty plain.

"That tree," Darcie says, downing the last of her mug's contents. "More coffee?"

The tree can't be less than three hundred meters away. "*That* one?" I point.

"Yeah. The only one. I'm getting more coffee, want some?"

"How the hell is Jules meant to hit that?"

Julian chuckles. "Oh, Jill. Sweet, innocent Jill. This isn't just some random gun for criminals and layabouts. This is a *military* gun."

Ben gives me a look. "It's a precision M28, pocket sniper model, with heat signature guidance. Helps you shoot human targets in the heart."

I feel slightly ill. "Then why is Jules shooting at a tree?"

"Do you see any other viable targets?" Julian says.

Ben stands and walks over to me. He continues to watch Julian with a critical eye but leans toward me so only I can hear his words. "I suggested we set up tin cans. Fleming wasn't interested. Wanted a *distant* target. I have a feeling they don't actually want to hit anything."

Oh, Julian. Soft-hearted, cantankerous Julian. I feel a sudden fondness for them, and I wonder if this is their way of bonding with Ben without admitting it.

Darcie reappears with coffee, handing me a mug. Ben returns to Julian's side, this time showing them how to safely load and unload a clip. The morning is quiet, chilly, but not so cold that I'm uncomfortable. I sip my coffee, and the warmth spreads through me pleasingly. We're in no great hurry today. The tech tent will take hours to set up, and it's important to get our bearings before we enter the field.

Darcie nudges me. "Ben's kinda hot when he's handling a gun."

"Is he?" I sip my coffee.

Darcie shoots me a look. "Oh, shut up. I know you're seeing those *arms* in that *tight t-shirt*."

"I maintain a professional opinion of each of my team-mates," I say.

"Yeah, okay, whatever. Don't think I didn't notice you two leaving the tent together last night."

I make a sound of incredulity. "Darce! We were talking."

"Uh-huh."

"I don't even *like* the guy."

"Then you won't mind if I...?" She smirks.

"Not at all," I say, taking a long sip of coffee, long enough that I have time to swallow my protest. "Have at it."

Darcie eyes me beadily but says nothing.

A soft ping cuts through the quiet morning.

Ben stands abruptly, looking at his watch. "Anomalous reading," he says. "Same as last night."

I move toward him, immediately interested. "From the same location?"

He nods, looking up at me. "I'm gonna check it out."

"I'll come," I offer, unthinking.

Julian sidles over, leaving the gun abandoned on its crate. "You guys were taking anomalous readings last night? *Alone?*"

"What did I *say*," Darcie whispers loudly.

"No, no," Ben says in response to my offer, waving me off. He ignores Julian and Darcie's insinuations, thank God. But the concern in his expression sets me on edge. "It's not far, just a few kliks. I'll be back well before lunchtime."

"Wait," Darcie says. "What is this anomaly? Why haven't we heard about it until now?"

"Because it might be nothing," Ben answers. "Listen, if any of you want to go out in the field while I'm gone, fine. But don't go alone. I still want to check the perimeters today before I okay solo work."

"Yeah, fine," Julian says, yawning. "Darce, you got any more of that coffee?"

She nods, and they head back to the main tent.

Ben and I are left alone together. He gathers up the gun, shoving it unceremoniously into a thigh holster. He turns and sees me watching. "What's up, Jones?"

I start, realizing I've been staring. "Oh, um. You sure you don't want me to come with you? I could use a walk."

He hesitates. I almost think he'll say yes. Then, "Nah. I could use the time alone. Try to rest today, yeah? See if there's more Napa wine to go with dinner." He grins, walks backward a few paces, then turns to stride out into the plain, the grasses following in his wake. Lazily, he puts out a hand, his palm brushing the grass.

I shiver, then shake my head to clear it. *He's not even my type.*

The sound of Darcie and Julian's bickering drifts toward me from the main tent, and I turn toward it, distracted. Maybe I'll have some breakfast and check out the lab tent. I'm sure most of the equipment must be old and probably needs cleaning at the very least. I brought most of what I'll need, but I'm curious to see what can be salvaged from the last expedition.

I go back to my tent and brush my teeth, then I shrug on my jacket and lace my boots up properly. I affix my walkie-talkie to my jacket and smooth my hair, tucking it behind my ears in a hopeless effort to feel put together. Grabbing a nutrient bar from my pack, I head out toward the lab tent.

A flock of birds rises from the tree line beyond camp, small shapes against the sky. If I didn't know any better, I'd think they were Earth birds. Not that I've ever seen those outside of recordings or shitty VR. But something deep inside me rises to meet the birds as they go, wishing I could reach up and hold their tails, let them take me somewhere far away. To the ocean's crashing waves, to the snow-encrusted mountaintops.

We're supposed to be taking samples, conducting tests. Scientific work to determine the Planet's viability. But aren't we explorers, too? Don't we deserve to feed our sense of wonder?

I pause, turning out toward the rippling plain. It's quiet. So green. It looks like a dream, a desire turned from pang to atom, forming and solidifying and laid out before me. How can I not be entranced? It's only for a second. I'll go to the lab tent after this.

Awash with something like euphoria, I walk out into the plain. Cool morning breeze greets me and lifts my hair, brushing the nape of my neck, my jaw, my face. I close my eyes, breathing deeply. This is the cleanest air I've ever tasted.

Further, further. I want to be surrounded by this.

I wonder if it was like this for my mother. Her expedition must not have been much different. They landed here when she was only twenty-three, the best botanist humanity had to offer. I wonder if she looked up at this same clear sky and felt tears gather at the corners of her eyes. If she touched the grass and felt infinite.

I walk slowly, knowing I should stay within sight of camp. But it's only for a minute. And who could blame me, the way the grass follows me, welcoming me just like the breeze? It kisses me gently. Cool beads of dew drip from bent blades, wetting my fingers.

Just a little further.

I just need a second.

7

JONES, *come in*.

The sun warms my face.

Jones.

I open my eyes, blinking against the light. Grasses rustle above me like a whispering forest. I'm on my back in the plain, gazing up at the sky.

Jones, come in.

Someone's talking to me, but their voice is staticky, muffled. Who could possibly want to pull me away from this? *This*, the ecstasy of my back pressed firmly against the living ground. I dig my fingers into the dirt and sigh. This, my skin against soil. This, the joy of life curving over me, grasses caressing my limbs, my cheeks, curling into me with abandon, unbound by propriety, by physics, by anything.

I sigh, languorous. I close my eyes and begin to decay.

It feels like the slow build to orgasm, the growing ache, tightness at my core, the knowing — impending blissful pleasure. Maggots rise up from the ground and consume me. My flesh rots away revealing sun-bleached bone. Fungi cluster at my softest spots, where the flesh is warm and bacteria-heavy.

Yes.

My body melts into the earth, inch by inch.

Jill Jones! Respond!

Ben's raised voice cuts through the haze of half-sleep and jolts me fully awake. I open my eyes again, and the sun blinds me, harsh. I sit up, arm over my face to block the too-bright light. I press my walkie-talkie with my thumb. "What?"

Jesus, don't scare me like that.

"Sorry." I run a thoughtless finger along a blade of grass, and it curls around me, all the way down to my wrist. "I fell asleep."

Fell asleep.

Something like that. "Weird dreams."

Weird dreams? Jones — What the hell did I say about going off alone? Stay there, I'm coming to you.

"No, don't bother, I'm fine." I study the dirt under my fingernails. What *was* I thinking, taking a nap in the middle of nowhere? I don't even remember lying down. If the weather turned... but the weather doesn't turn here. There are no surprise storms, no flash floods. No stealthy predators. Just mild days and crisp nights, the perfect conditions. Always.

I'm a quarter klick from your position. I'll be there in a second.

"What the hell is a klick?"

It's a kilometer.

I stand up, turn, and see Ben's figure striding through the grass toward me. I wave, but he doesn't wave back. He's supposed to be off to the north, investigating that anomaly. Why is he out here bothering me?

He arrives with a sour look on his face and gives me a disapproving once-over. "Are you sick or something?"

"No, why?" I glance down, brushing specks of dirt from my jacket. "I got tired, drifted off for like a second. Aren't you supposed to be checking out that energy spike?"

He gives me the strangest look. "I did check it out. Hours ago. I went back to camp, and you weren't there. The others hadn't seen you."

I check my watch. Fuck. I *was* asleep for hours. I glance at the sun, and — it's already past midday. I thought it was still morning. "Oh."

"Oh," echoes Ben, obviously displeased. "You can't disappear for hours on an alien planet. Especially not in direct violation of an order."

His distress lights a pleased, defiant little fire in me. He's not my boss. Not technically. "Sorry, *sir*."

He closes his eyes for a long second, like he's already so done with this shit. "Don't call me sir."

"Whatever you say, Dad."

"Not *that*, either."

I bite the inside of my mouth to stop myself from this shameless flirting. I don't know *why* I want to push every one of his buttons right now. Who is he, though, to tell me what to do? Just because he has a gun. I hold his gaze defiantly. "You had my location the whole time."

He moves toward me, his jaw tight. "You weren't responding to my communications. You could've been dead for all I knew."

I think of the dream, the slow sink into my grave. It felt

good. Beautiful. Right. "What if I did?" I say, staring past his shoulder at the plain beyond, the dark smudge that is the forest, and the pale purple-blue hints of mountain beyond that. "I'd rather do it here than on a ship."

"Okay, spooky, we're going back to camp now." He radios the others, letting them know I'm safe and that we're heading back. He puts a firm hand between my shoulder blades, urging me forward. "Let's go. There's something you need to see."

I stop walking. There's something in his tone that feels like a bruise being pressed. "You found the source of the anomaly?"

He turns to me. "Yeah. But it's—"

"What is it?"

He won't meet my gaze. Then he sighs, screwing up his face like he's losing a fight with himself. "In the plain to the north, I found a piece of equipment left behind by your mother's expedition."

I blink, all my pointless defiance gone. "The entire camp is full of equipment they left behind."

He rubs the back of his neck, squinting up at the sky. "This one belonged to your mom."

A stone settles in my gut. "Oh."

"It's nothing, it's a walkie-talkie. But I thought you should have it. It's back at camp if you want to—"

"Why was it out there?" I ask, like he'll even begin to know. My mother dropped it, obviously. In some kind of fit. Or a panic. While running from something. *To* something. It could be any reason, none of them nice.

He finally catches my gaze again and softens. "Listen,

Jones, I can't begin to guess. And frankly, we'll never know. But something's stumping me."

I nod. "How it could have been emitting that energy spike."

"Bingo. I haven't checked it out yet, but it's a miracle if the battery's even running."

"Yeah," I say, distracted. I brush my knuckles against the grass, a thoughtless act of comfort, and the grass caresses me in return.

"Let's head back," Ben says with finality. "The others are worried about you. We can look at your mom's walkie more closely if you—"

"I don't," I interrupt. The thought of it makes me sick. "I mean, not yet. I'm still..."

He pats my back, two sharp slaps, a straight male platonic showing of support. "Got it. No need to explain."

Somehow, his lack of curiosity bothers me. Doesn't he want to know? The rest of the world seemingly can't get enough gossip about my mom. "It's just strange," I say, staring out at the grass.

Ben looks at me. "Yeah?"

"Being here. Knowing she was here. And not even knowing exactly what happened, outside of what was in the news."

He rests his weight on one leg, crossing his arms. "She never told you."

I shake my head. He's going to make some snide remark, now. Or ask what I think happened, or try to dig deeper into my mother's trauma.

But he just sighs. "I know you don't wanna talk about it.

And I won't ask you to. But I know what it's like to walk out of Hell and get an ice-cold welcome from the people who are supposed to be on your side. Whatever happened here, all those years ago, your mom's a victim. And so are you."

I bristle. "I'm not—"

"I *mean* it's okay to feel like shit," he says, putting up a hand in placation. "Even in this gorgeous place."

My defenses recede, and I realize I'm close to tears, startled by his understanding. In all my thirty-one years, I've never been allowed to feel the way I want to feel about my mom. It's always been about how I *should* feel, that I should be proud, or grateful, or ashamed.

Ben slaps his thigh with one hand. "Welp, shall we?"

I can't help but smile. "We shall."

We walk side by side back to camp. We're further out than I remember going, and I'm vibrating with the fact that I'm alone with Ben. I glance sideways at him. His gaze is straight ahead, but every once in a while, he surveys the area, a habit burned into him for life, I suspect. He keeps his hand near his sidearm, one thumb hooked in the pocket of his cargoes, fingers hanging inches away from the weapon at his thigh.

"What do you think you'll have to shoot out here?" I ask. I genuinely want to know.

He sighs, a staccato exhale that almost feels like a laugh. "If you make a joke about trees..."

"No, I'm curious. Do you *have* to carry it?"

"Yes."

"By law?"

His mouth twitches in a half-smile. I'm quietly triumphant; I like surprising him. "It's for our safety."

"To protect us from the rodents."

"Yes."

We're quiet for a few moments. "What about the grass?"

He frowns, glancing at me. "Grass?"

I hold out my hands, palms down, caressing the curving green sea with my skin. He watches, still frowning, and comes to a stop. I stop too, watching him. Hasn't he noticed it? Hasn't he felt it following us, angling eagerly toward us? I drink in his expression as something clicks into place.

"It's... moving," he says, holding out one hand. The grass shivers, reacting to his touch the same way it reacts to all of us: with hungry reverence. He turns his hand over, running his knuckles along the green, and my breath catches. I can almost feel it, the coarseness of his hands, his calloused palms against my skin.

I watch as his expression turns from confusion to disbelief, and then a soft awe.

"Well, fuck me," he says. "It's beautiful."

There's wonder in his voice. His words hit me like last night's wine, making me light-headed and warm. In a rush of near-madness, I find I want to press my lips to his, to inhale that praise like it's mine.

"How?" he asks.

"I don't know," I breathe. "I haven't tested it yet. But I think it's similar to this species of fern back on Earth that reacts to physical touch."

He raises his eyebrows. "It's not dangerous, is it?"

My gaze falls to his hands again. He's still fingering the lush blades of grass, his expression thoughtful, like he wants to understand it on a cellular level. It occurs to me that this isn't objectively sexy. It's a man touching grass. But as he runs one finger along a particularly eager length of silver-green, I *swear* I feel it. I don't have to imagine the sensation of his hand, warm and firm, roving up from my waist to my ribs. I feel his thumb brush against the under-side of my breast, and with a sharp inhale, I—

"All right, come on," Ben says. "I'm starving. Haven't eaten since breakfast."

I snap back to reality, humiliation pooling in my gut. I'm having vivid fantasies about what amounts to my boss because he's interested in *grass*. I should've gotten laid before we left.

"Yeah," I say, my face hot.

But Ben doesn't notice, or he does and decides not to comment. I'm grateful either way.

By the time we return to camp, Julian and Darcie are expanding the already large dent in the wine store. The main tent's flap is pinned open, and it smells like Darcie's cooking something.

Before we reach the tent, Ben touches my arm, stopping me in my tracks. "I know you won't, but just... don't go out alone again. Not until I've cleared it. Got me?"

I nod, acutely aware of where his fingers just brushed my sleeve. "Yeah, got you."

He huffs. "Just... pretend I'm your senior officer for two seconds."

A shiver runs down my body. "Yes, sir."

He grins. "Good. Now let's go see what's on tap for lunch."

I follow in his wake, hating that the more I call him *sir*, the more I like it.

8

LUNCH BUZZES WITH ANTICIPATORY ENERGY. We're itching to explore, to start collecting samples and performing tests. So far, all we've seen is grass, sky, the distant forest, and the even more distant mountains. It turns out Darcie and Julian spent the rest of their morning setting up the lab tent and cooking.

Our meal is a simple affair of leftover stew, more vegetable essence, and canned bread. I refrain from asking Darcie what the fuck canned bread is, wondering how long such a thing could possibly last without refrigeration. Everyone's enjoying the wine except for me.

As much as I don't want to, I can't stop thinking about my mother's walkie. Why would she have left it out there? Was she attacked? Was it wrenched from her? I dwell on the moments between what's on the public record; the cracks where things can fall and become hidden for decades.

"Hey," Darcie says, elbowing me softly. Ben and Julian are bickering animatedly about guns, a subject about which

Julian now feels they are an expert, much to Ben's obvious irritation. Darcie's presence is suddenly intimate and kind, her attention reserved just for me. "You good?"

I know what she's really asking. *How are you feeling after wandering into the plain and having a dissociative episode, no doubt due to the emotional turmoil of returning to the alien land that forever broke your mother, and, in turn, you?*

For a wild moment, I consider answering honestly: That I'm feeling like shit. I think of the grass against my skin. The way I felt while I thought I was sinking into the earth, decaying, and I'm sick, nauseous, but at the same time... it's like a crooked line falling into place. I look at the mosaic of my life, and for once, it's a full, vibrant image, growing brighter by the second. Never mind that the image is laced with dread, with truths I don't want to know.

"Yeah," I say, smiling. "I think maybe the hypersleep is still hanging over me. Never agreed with me."

"No," Darcie says, searching my face. "Never did."

"And you?" I ask, a sudden needle of aggravation spurring me onward. Why should I be the one everyone worries about? We're all lonely, all troubled. "You left some heavy shit behind on Earth."

Darcie sits back. "You *know* I don't want to talk about—"

"Back me up here," Julian cuts in obliviously, leaning across the table, already wine-sloppy in the middle of the day. "We should be allowed to take turns with G-dawg, right?"

Darcie and I stare.

Ben shakes his head, like he's washing his hands of this.

"The gun," Julian explains, in the tone of someone talking down to a pair of infants. "G-dawg."

Darcie reaches for her wine. "Right, so we're not getting any more work done today."

"Jules," I say, leaning forward as if we're having an intimate one-on-one despite the immediate presence of Darcie and Ben. "You want to take turns doing *what* with G—... with the gun?"

"G-dawg."

"No," says Darcie.

"I can't say it," I laugh.

Ben sighs.

Julian fixes me with a withering glare, but the wine softens their expression until it fades into a smile. "Carrying it. Wielding it. Taking *care* of it. It's only fair."

Ben leans forward, arms crossed at the elbow on the tabletop. "Fair? Who said anything about fair?"

Julian swings to face Ben, their movements overly dramatic, loose. They flick Ben on the shoulder with long fingers. "Well, what if I'm alone in the field, and I'm attacked. Who's going to save me? You? You, Benjamin, who is busy several *klicks* away trying to get into Jill's—"

"Okay," I cut in, grabbing Julian's wine and sliding it out of arm's reach. "That's enough Napa juice for J-Dawg."

Darcie covers her mouth, obviously laughing and trying to hide it with a cough.

Julian, not sparing a glance for their confiscated wine, fixes Ben with a pleading gaze and clasps their hands together as if praying. Their glasses fall down their nose, and they push them back up. "It's only fair. Three hours each, every day. I'll be so good to the lethal little guy."

"I think I prefer Jules when they're sauced," Darcie says, just for me.

Ben closes his eyes, sighs, and opens them a moment later as if he's hoping Julian will have disappeared in the interim. "Finish your wine, Fleming. And then take a nap."

Julian flops into a sulk. "Guess you want me to die."

"Guess so," mutters Ben.

Darcie shoots me a look. A look that says she's still hung up on the *Trying to get into Jill's* line. The way we both saw a muscle in Ben's jaw flutter when Julian spoke, and we both know it.

I shoot *her* a look that says, *Don't you dare say a word, or I'll end you.*

She only smiles.

"Listen," Ben says, clearly fed up with everything and everyone, "I'm gonna check out the forest before it gets dark. *With* G-dawg," he adds in response to Julian's hopeful glance. "Based on all the readings, it should be biologically and geographically safe. But I'm gonna confirm that myself before I let you three loose in there on your own, only to fall in an unmapped ravine. Stay in camp while I'm gone, got it? Enjoy the rest of the day. Tomorrow, we're getting some goddamn work done."

"Okay, boss," Julian says, putting up a sloppy salute.

"Thank you," I say, immediately regretting it. *Thank you?* God, what's wrong with me?

"I thought you didn't even *like* him," Darcie murmurs under her breath as Ben moves toward the exit.

Julian leans across the table, retrieving their wine from where I've been holding it hostage, and takes a massive swig. "Why's he safe to go in the forest? What is he, like, immune to ravines or something?"

A low voice cuts in. "Jones?" Ben's hovering just inside the tent.

I start, my heart pounding. Can everyone see the hot blood racing in my veins? I raise my eyebrows, questioning.

He jerks his head toward the deepening afternoon. "Come on, I need to show you that thing."

Ah. The walkie. Part of me wanted to forget about it; pretend it hadn't been found. On paper, I'm here for progress, for humanity. I don't want or need these relics from a parent's life I barely know, a parent whose experiences I had to piece together from news clips and prime-time interviews. But still...

I get up and follow him, knowing the looks Darcie and Julian are sharing right now, and dreading the moment they'll get me alone to grill me and tease me about it. I get it; they're buzzing on adrenaline and nerves and excitement, and they need somewhere to direct that energy. And maybe, yeah, so do I. But it's nothing. It's just a silly cru—

My thoughts short-circuit as I realize where we are. Ben holds open the flap to his own tent, motioning me inside. I freeze. *Is this about the walkie?*

He catches my gaze, and several micro-expressions flit across his face before he settles on an unreadable half-smile. "Your mother's walkie is in my tent. You can stay out here if you want, just have to grab it."

"Right," I say, heart in my throat.

I follow him inside the tent. The top of his head brushes the canvas. It's close in here, warmer than outside, but not uncomfortably so. He reaches up and flicks on the lantern, filling the shadows with warm light. We're feet away from each other, but his body heat seems to envelop me.

"Here we go," he says, crouching down and opening the trunk at the foot of his cot. He pulls something out, closes the trunk, stands, and holds out his hand. There it is: the most nondescript walkie-talkie I've ever seen. The technology hasn't changed in decades. It's a bit retro, but otherwise, it's just like our walkies.

I stare down at the device. My mother held that with her warm fingers, the breath from her mouth hot against its black surface, right here on this planet. Maybe even in this tent. What damning words did she utter against this object? What fear did she express? Was it ever anything worth keeping, or even throwing away? Was it worth all the silence she knitted between us, year after year?

"Jones?"

I snap back to the present moment. Ben's broad hand, holding the walkie out toward me. His palms are calloused, his fingers long but blunt, like he's just as good at punching as he is at reloading a rifle at record speed. Not that loading rifles or punching is hot. It's stupid, chauvinistic, and unappealing.

He clears his throat.

"Sorry," I blurt, taking the walkie and turning it over in my hands. "It's just... seeing this here..." I frown, looking up at him. His gaze is soft, concerned like I've never seen it before, and my legs consider crumpling. I try to think of something to say. "How do you know it's hers?"

He reaches out. "May I?"

I nod.

He turns the walkie in my loose grip, his rough fingers brushing mine, until a small round label comes into view: Jones.

My knees almost give out again for a different reason. This is becoming all too real. My mother, this planet, everything that happened here. All the things we still don't know. What if all the worst things they say about her are true? That she's nothing better than a murderer? That her team's disappearance wasn't mysterious at all, that *she* killed them?

"Jones, you okay?"

I swallow rising nausea. "Mmhmm. Thank you. I'm gonna go." I turn to leave.

Ben's fingers fasten on my upper arm, holding me back. "Are you sure? If you're having a rough time, we can—"

I spin to face him. Shake my head. "Thank you. No. I'm good."

I can't get out of there fast enough. The walkie feels infinitely heavy in my hand. A time-bomb. A tactile connection to a truth I don't want to contemplate. I know enough about this place, what happened, to know that I'd rather not touch it. Or feel it.

My mind goes to Andrews. It always does when I'm not in control of my thoughts. How she and my mom were close, how they'd sneak off together to be alone. And how Andrews disappeared one day, and my mom found her deep in the forest. I never asked my mom about it, but I'd seen her respond to questions about Andrews, their relationship, in the interviews. She never liked talking about Andrews. Of all the things she experienced on the Planet,

Andrews was the one subject that disturbed my mother most.

I don't want to wonder about what happened to Andrews.

When I get to my tent, I don't bother turning on the lantern. I fall to my knees, ignoring the pain. My hands are shaking now, my breaths shallow. I shove the walkie under my cot, away, into the inky shadows. It thuds and rolls once, then falls still.

"And fucking stay there."

I feel something soft under my hands. I glance down, and my breath catches. I hadn't seen in the dim light — there are tiny green seedlings all over the floor. They've burst up through the canvas bottom of the tent, growing all around the feet of the cot. I pluck one seedling, holding it up to my face. It's just a plant. A small, delicate thing.

I stand, still unsteady, and take a long, deep breath. I let the seedling fall from my fingers. This place is stressing me out. I need a fucking distraction, and not the Ben kind.

9

JULIAN IS sober by the time they join me in the lab tent, hours later. Dusk falls over the campsite, and twin moons paint the plain in silvery hues. It looks like a sea of mercury through the shitty tent windows, plasticky and warped as they are.

"Need some help?" Julian asks, face half-obscured by curtains of hair.

I'm in the middle of tinkering with a centrifuge. It's got some kind of balance issue, and I can't get it to spin right. "Nah," I say. "Did you get a nap?"

"Yes, Mom."

I shoot them a look. "Doesn't it get exhausting?"

"What?"

"Being an obnoxious prick all the time."

"Not at all," they say airily, coming to watch me pry open the centrifuge with an old screwdriver. "It's invigorating, actually. Your expressions of derision delight me in ways I can't begin to express."

"Uh-huh. At least it's distracting you from G-dawg."

Julian makes a face. "Who?"

"Christ. Never mind. Wanna give me a hand with this, actually?" I hold out the screwdriver. "I can't get the bottom piece loosened."

Julian takes the screwdriver wordlessly and begins daintily working at the same screw that was giving me trouble. I watch, half-focused on the scrape of metal on metal, half-focused on the undulation of the grass outside the window. It's beautiful beyond description. Nothing like that ever existed on Earth.

"So what's the deal with Ben?" Julian asks, still poking away with the screwdriver.

All my attention is on them now. "What do you mean?"

They shoot me a glance, brow raised. "Oh, I think you know. What was '*I need to show you that thing*' all about? *His* thing?"

"Shut up, that was—" I reach desperately for an explanation and come up short. "That was nothing."

"So you *didn't* go back to his tent and copulate?"

"*Copulate*? Oh my God, Jules, everything you say is so—"

"Correct?" They purse their lips. "I know."

"I was going to say infuriating."

They shrug. "Hmm. I only ask because I thought we all decided he was a doofus."

"I must have missed that meeting." I did think he was a doofus. I still do. I *do*.

"It wasn't a *meeting*, it is the natural state of physics, biology, and the universe. Intelligent, thoughtful women of science don't waste their time with men who perform push-ups as a mating ritual."

I snort, despite myself. "I've never once seen Ben do a push-up."

Julian looks up, eyes narrowing. "But you *have* imagined it."

"No—"

"You *have*!" they declare, triumphant, pointing the screwdriver at me. "Ha! Slumming it, pal. You're a real squalid individual, you know that? I'd put money on him not even knowing where the clitoris is located."

"Fuck *off*, Jules."

"I bet he doesn't even know what it *is*." Julian chuckles, going back to uselessly jamming the screwdriver against the stuck screw. "Do you think he's ever made a woman come before? Want me to educate him? I can whip together a slideshow within a quarter hour, easy. *How to gently fuck J*—"

"Shut *up*," I snap, snatching the screwdriver from Julian's grasp. "You're pissing me off now. This is beyond unprofessional."

Julian gives me a withering look. "Right, and this is such a buttoned-up, by-the-book expedition."

"What's that supposed to mean?" I go back to fiddling with the centrifuge. I think it must be rusted; we'll need something more than a screwdriver to fix it.

"Don't tell me you haven't thought about it. Considering the situation, I mean."

I pause and meet their gaze. "What situation?"

"Well, take into account your mother's failed expedition, for one. The ramifications. The fact that *you're* here. I mean, haven't you once asked yourself the important questions? Like why the ECE spent millions to send a team of explorers back to the Planet, and they picked *us* of all people?"

I roll my eyes. Not another conspiracy theory. "Whatever you say, flat-earther. I'm more than qualified to be on this mission. I campaigned for years to get it off the ground."

"No doubt, no doubt. All I'm saying is, look at this team. Every last one of us should be in a mental institution. But here we are, wandering around on an alien planet, gathering... I guess plant and water samples, or whatever."

I let out a long breath. I set down the screwdriver and plant my hands on the table, palms down. "Spit it out. What's your theory? They're going to start sending crazy people to planets now instead of asylums? We're the test run?"

"*Crazy* is a slur," Julian says primly. "And no, why on God's brown Earth would they send all of our freaks to the one planet that might be viable for human colonization?"

"And *freak* isn't a slur?"

"No, no. We're not here to stay, not on paper anyway. But we're also, shall we say, isolated individuals. Loners, if you catch my drift. I mean, did you have a single friend before training started?"

I stiffen, making a sound of protestation. Where the hell is Julian going with this?

"Mm. Thought not. Now let's imagine if something... *befell* us on the Planet."

"Let's not and say we did."

Julian holds my stare, their glasses glinting in the lamplight. "Just think about it. Who would even attend our funerals? You're a classic case of CPTSD, Jill Jones. I'm a deeply depressed individual with narcissistic tendencies. Darcie... well, we both know what she's been through. What I'm curious about, though, is our intrepid soldier. What, do you suppose, is deeply psychologically wrong with *Benjamin*?"

"Someone called?" Ben's voice cuts in from the lab entrance.

I glare at Julian, irritated at how easily they can unsettle me. "Ben, can you help us with uh, the centrifuge?"

Julian watches me, smiling. Sometimes I wish I could punch them and not hurt my knuckles doing it.

Ben strides in, his jacket open, thumbs hooked in the pockets of his cargoes. He takes in the scene. "You're gonna break it," he says.

"What do you know of esoteric lab equipment?" asks Julian.

"I know a centrifuge is not *esoteric*, for one."

Julian makes an impressed sort of grunt. I stare at the screwdriver.

"Come on, team meeting in the main tent," Ben says. He goes to the entrance, then turns back when nobody responds. "Now."

The three of us traipse through the camp, the dusk now thickening to true evening. A navy blue blanket of night hangs over us, scattered with so many stars. I'll never get used to this clear air, the newness of it. Is this how Earth used to be? Or is that a myth, an imaginary children's story, and *this* is the real planet? The real beauty?

Ben holds the flap to the main tent, and we duck into the warm light. Darcie is already seated at the table. She smiles, but her usual cheerful demeanor has faded. I've seen it a dozen times. She lapses, sometimes, into a personal darkness.

"Right, let's make this quick," says Ben when we've all taken a seat at the table. He's in full leader mode, hands on hips, brows drawn low. "Nobody wants to listen to me ramble about *rules*, so here's the quick and dirty."

I can feel Julian's sideways glance and pointedly ignore it.

"The forest is safe to traverse, technically," Ben continues. "But I still don't like the idea of anyone leaving camp alone. You're to go out in pairs and report in every hour, on the hour."

All three of us make a collective sound of incredulity.

"But there's only three of us," Darcie protests. "So we'd always be going out as a trio."

"You're stifling my scientific process and creative expression," Julian adds.

Ben holds up a hand for silence. "In case you forgot, I exist. I'm happy to join any of you in the field if you need a buddy."

I brace for a humiliating comment from Julian or Darcie, but they're both too wrapped up in their protestation to think of embarrassing me.

"Do you have the authority to make this call?" Darcie asks, her expression mask-like. "I thought this mission was cleared before launch. So what, did you find something weird in the forest?"

"A ravine?" Julian suggests. "A bunny rabbit?"

A muscle in Ben's jaw flexes. "I *do* have the authority to make this call. I'm happy to direct you to the fine print in your mission handbooks. Listen, this is only temporary. A few days at most, until I'm satisfied the field is safe for solo work."

I keep my mouth shut. I have long since learned there's no point in raising a fuss over something out of my control. I don't like Ben's tone or the bite of his words. Right now, he's not our friend, not our teammate. He's our boss. And he'll enforce whatever rules he lays down if he has to.

And I *hate* that Ben exercising his authority does it for me.

There's continued grumbling, but nobody puts up a fight. Julian's probably still worn out from their day drinking, and Darcie is obviously having an episode. I'd ask her if she's okay, if she needs anything, but I already know how she'd react: badly.

"Okay," says Ben, clapping his hands together. "That's it, gang. Remember, teams of two!"

"Yeah, yeah," Darcie mutters, getting up from the table and drifting away.

"You think she'll still cook dinner?" Julian hisses in my ear.

"I will if you keep your trap shut," Darcie calls over her shoulder.

Julian does a fist pump.

I think of Andrews, deep in the forest, utterly alone, and I'm quietly relieved.

10

OVER THE NEXT THREE DAYS, we fall into a routine. We wake up, have breakfast, and then venture into the Planet's untamed wilderness. We never go far — we're only able to travel at walking speed, after all. But once we make our assessments, in time, more people will come, and more, until the entire planet is mapped out and categorized: Habitable, Uninhabitable, Other. For three whole days, we carefully avoid the topic of my mom. For three whole days, Julian doesn't piss me off.

It's almost like the Planet's beauty makes us softer, soothes us. It's difficult to be irritated, I find, when I'm kilometers deep in a sea of grass, the soil at my feet, both my palms pressed to the bark of a tree. It's difficult to think about my mom's walkie when I'm dipping my bare feet in ice-cold glacier runoff, gasping at the sensation, screaming when Darcie splashes me and runs off, laughing.

Darcie's darkness dissipates over those three days. I see it in the way she smiles at the grass coiling around her fingers. I see it in the way she breathes, watching a flock of birds make their way toward the distant snow-capped peaks.

The days are sweet, quiet. We laugh, sitting in the grass, which is so tall it forms a sort of sphere around us, shading us from the sun. She teases me about Ben. I act embarrassed. But out here, under the sky, with growing things all around us, I can't be angry. It's almost impossible. It's all too new, and radiant, and real.

Even Julian and Ben seem to be finding common ground. Every morning they practice with the gun, and every morning Ben refuses to let Julian carry it into the field. They return from their ventures in the forest, joking and laughing.

Ben and I don't spend much time together, not one-on-one. He's probably heard the others making little comments, seen the way Darcie shoots me knowing smiles when we're together. And it's easier to avoid him, to focus on the work, on studying plant cells under a microscope. It's easier to just pretend I don't feel a sharp, wanting pang in the middle of my chest whenever he looks at me.

It's okay, though. The Planet is why I'm here. She is the reason I studied botany, why I insisted this mission go forward, why I signed up for a spot. We could make all this work. This could be the one. Maybe, I think, this is humanity's salvation.

I don't think about my mother until I'm in my cot, eyes closed against the night. I try not to think about Andrews, or what I saw in my mother's eyes when she spoke of her lover. But Andrews comes to me anyway, in my dreams.

And in those raw, miserable moments, retching over the edge of my cot, cold sweat soaking my sheets, I wonder if *this* isn't what's real after all.

11

ON OUR FIFTH night on the Planet, we get drunk again.

It's another sort of celebration — we made it this far, to an arbitrary number of days, and why shouldn't we toast to that? Darcie lays out a fantastic spread: a roasted lump of lab-grown canned chicken product, the essence of various vegetables, more canned bread, and even something that is so close in texture and flavor to mashed potatoes, that I'm momentarily stunned after my first bite.

"Pretty good for a bunch of weird old food, huh?" Darcie says, holding up her cup, wine sloshing dangerously close to the edges.

"It's better than what I ate back on Earth," says Ben.

Julian splutters. "The consummate bachelor, Benjamin is."

Ben smiles, holding his wine to his lips. "Who has time for cooking when you're busy doing push-ups for eight hours a day?"

"See?" Julian says, slamming down their fork and

sending a chunk of chicken product careening away into the shadows. "I knew it."

"He's mocking *you*," Darcie says laughingly. "Nobody does push-ups eight hours a day."

"My arms would be bigger than my torso," says Ben.

I listen to them, happy in this moment, on this quiet planet with three people whose friendship wasn't chosen but happened all the same. I'm full of good wine and good *enough* food, and everything's gone soft at the edges. Their voices fade and become a comforting background blur as I sip my wine, lost in my thoughts.

Until Darcie ruins it.

"Wait, you know that one?" Darcie declares, standing abruptly and jostling me out of my peaceful thoughts.

I grab my cup to keep it from spilling.

Julian scoffs. "Do I *know* it? Bitch, I used to play it every weekend. I was the champion. What do you think we even do in graduate programs?"

"I might have guessed *study*," says Darcie.

"How uninspired," Julian says. "We had all sorts of drinking games to amuse us."

"Well?" says Darcie, pouring herself another cup of wine. "Are we gonna go play it or not?"

They're already sloshed. Darcie spills a significant amount of priceless Napa reserve on the table, and Julian cackles, holding out their cup for a refill. And then the two are off, gingerly carrying their overfull cups of wine, talking loudly, and laughing as if it really is grad school again.

I'm painfully, hotly aware that Ben and I are suddenly alone.

I glance at him, feeling inexplicably shy. I meet his gaze for a fleeting breath, and then he looks away.

"You should join them," he says, and I'm not sure if it's my imagination, but his voice sounds more gravelly than usual.

"I don't know the game." Whatever game they're playing, I definitely never partook in grad school. "I was more of a... what do you call it? Complete loser in university."

Ben laughs. "Couldn't have been worse than me."

I turn to face him, leaning one elbow on the table. My heart is pounding a mile a minute. "Oh yeah? You, too, skipped going out on weekends with friends to get in some extra reading on the viability of long-term hydroponics in zero-gravity environments?"

"No, but that sounds fascinating."

I can't help the pleased little smile that curls my lips. He's watching me so intently, as if he's actually interested. "Okay, now you're just sucking up. I don't believe for a second that you weren't the most adored guy in school, all the way through college. I mean—" I cut myself off. I was going to say *look at you*, but I catch myself at the last second. Fucking wine.

A peel of drunken laughter drifts in from outside. Darcie and Julian are fully caught up in their game.

Ben eyes me, a smirk curling one corner of his mouth. "Have you heard of BattleAxe?"

"The tabletop strategy game?"

"Yeah, the one for nerds." He grins. "All me, baby. Could not drag me away from that game. All the way from age twelve to twenty-three. I had the biggest army. Took me years to build it, all funded by a part-time job at the local diner."

"Stop," I breathe, completely charmed.

"What can I say?" He holds up his hands. "I was a loser."

I lean forward, conspiratorial. "Do you still play?"

He narrows his eyes. "That's classified information."

I laugh, and he brightens. I sip my wine. My heart is still on high alert, my skin on fire, but it's muffled now. The wine is doing its work. Good. I need to relax, get hold of myself. This torch I've been carrying for him for a year needs to be snuffed out. Nothing can come of Ben and me. He's too good for me.

He sips his wine and runs a hand through his short hair. His gaze strays, and suddenly, I don't want him to decide that now's a good time to turn in for the night. It's late, but I selfishly want to keep him for a little longer. Even if it's just to talk.

"What about you?" I ask, and his brows pull together in slight confusion. I realize I'm continuing a conversation that took place days ago. "Why did you sign up for the mission? It can't be that fulfilling, wrangling a trio of scientists."

He shrugs, holding my gaze warmly. "Lots of reasons. But I guess... well, mostly I wanted to get away from it all. I felt like I'd seen the best Earth had to offer, which wasn't much, and this opportunity came up. So I took it."

Another burst of laughter from outside and a loud curse from Julian.

Ben smiles. "You know, they remind me of my siblings. Idiots, all of them, but good people. Lots of potential." He stares into the middle distance, and his smile fades a bit. "I enlisted for them, really. When I was twenty-four. I'm the middle kid, but my older brother's an artist, couldn't make a solid living if it killed him. My younger sister's just an asshole, quits every job she gets. Back then, I knew I was the only one of us who had the sense to hold down a solid career. And I was never that great at math, or science, or anything else." He glances up at me and smiles, almost sheepish. "But I am good at shooting."

"I've yet to see it," I say, touching his arm so briefly I'm sure he didn't even feel it. I can't *help* it. He's telling me a vulnerable story about his life, but I can't drag my eyes away from his jaw, his bare neck, where his dog tags fall against his chest.

"I'll show you," he says quietly.

"That's why you joined the military," I say, suddenly realizing I need to steer this conversation in another direction, or it'll be too late. "But why this mission, of all missions? There are other off-world explorations. Mars?"

"God of war?" Ben says, shaking his head. "Nah, not my thing. Too close to home."

His gaze is shadowed. There's something he won't say. Normally, I'd leave him with his memories. But the wine forces me to ask, softly, "What's so bad that you had to be trillions of miles away from it?"

He lets out a long sigh. "Nothing you'd want to hear about."

"Try me."

I think he might brush me off, stand up, and go back to his tent. But he meets my gaze, and something he sees there holds him. "I was an officer at The Three Follies."

I can't help the intake of breath. That battle was a massacre. Almost everyone died, chalked up to bad leadership.

"Yeah, you know it," he says ruefully. "I wasn't the acting general, of course. But I had authority. I had a say. And I led my men straight into a trap. Everyone died but me and two others. I'm fucking lucky to be whole after that. And when I came back home to the grand old U.S. of A., I was reviled in military circles. Treated like a traitor. They think I meant to do it."

"Of course you didn't."

He smiles crookedly. "Of course I didn't. But you know how it goes. Someone picks an angle, and that's what the news runs with. They needed a scapegoat."

We share a look that says he knows I'm thinking of my mother, and he gets it, and he knows I understand him. My heart swells. "I can't believe I didn't realize that was you," I breathe. "I mean... I'm barely tuned into foreign affairs, but..."

"No, no," he says, mussing his hair with his hand again. "I'm glad you're not. It's part of the reason I wanted to join the mission. This one, specifically. A small group, none of them military."

I smile, and he smiles back. "You shouldn't have worried," I murmur. "You're way more interesting with a dark backstory."

"Oh yeah?" He lets his arm fall to the table. If he moved it inward, just a few inches, he could cup my elbow in his hand. Run his thumb along my sleeve. "And what about you, Jones?"

I swallow roughly. If I leaned forward, just a little, I

could almost press my lips to his. "What about me?"

"You think I don't find you fascinating?" His arm slides toward me. His thumb brushes my sleeve. "The way you think, your optimism, your intellect. It's... intimidating."

"Intimidating?"

"In a good way."

Time seems to slow. There's an undeniable energy between us, an electrical pull. Blood roars in my veins. I can't stop looking at his mouth. His gaze, too, flickers down. Is he thinking what I am? Does he want to know what it would feel like to quench the ache inside me, the one I suspect might be in him, too?

Laughter and loud voices cut through the night. Darcie and Julian burst into the tent.

"And *then* I said, like fuck you'll call me Joo-Joo!" Julian crows.

"Nooohoho!" Darcie cackles, face pink with night air and wine and laughter.

They both stop dead as Ben and I sit back abruptly, turning away from each other.

Darcie nudges Julian. "Ssh, if you stay quiet and don't move, they'll forget we're here."

"No, they won't," I say, standing up and pushing away from the table. "You'd alert anyone within miles to your presence with those piercing cackles. Enjoy your game, I'm going to bed."

Still unspeakably breathless, wanting, unable to think straight, I hurry from the tent and into the night. I have *got* to stop indulging in that Napa stuff; it makes me unbelievably stupid. Head down, I make a beeline for my tent.

Embarrassed and frustrated, I'm just outside my tent when footsteps come up behind me.

"Jones," he says.

I stop, but I don't turn to face him.

"You okay?"

"I'm fine," I manage, hoping I don't sound completely fucking horny. I can feel his warmth at my back. He's standing so close.

"You went pale and ran away," he says softly. "I'm sorry if... if I gave you some kind of impression. It wasn't intentional."

I exhale slowly. The night is chill and clean, the Milky Way spread out above us like silver embroidery on velvet. *It wasn't intentional.* Maybe, maybe not. But what I do next is.

12

I TAKE A STEP BACK, turning my head just enough so he knows that I see him, that I can feel how close he is. His jacket, unzipped, brushes against my back. His breath ruffles my hair. He inhales like he's about to speak. No, shut up, Ben.

Another step back.

A sharp intake of breath.

His dog tags press against my back, cold through my shirt. His chest rises and falls, warm against my shoulder blades. I tilt my chin up, looking back, and see that his eyes are closed, brows drawn together. Is he disgusted? Trying to think of a way to get out of this moment, this intimacy?

But before I can decide how to react, he decides for me. He grabs my hips, slowly and deliberately.

I stifle a quiet gasp.

A chilly wind cools my face. The crickets, which we now know are amphibious, chirp a faint song for the night.

Ben pulls me closer until there's no space between us.

He holds me there with one hand on my belly. The other drifts down, down to the hem of my shirt, which he pulls up with gentle fingers. My eyes flutter shut. He holds me steady, helpless against his chest, his heartbeat a staccato of desire.

I'm in a senseless state of need when he unbuttons my cargoes. When he lowers the zipper, centimeter by centimeter.

I'm light-headed, breathing too fast when he lowers his mouth to my ear. I could erupt into flames. I could let the sky pull me into its infinite depths, dragging me apart, atom by atom. I could let the grasses pull me in, caressing, enfolding, until there's nothing left. I could dematerialize. I'm ready to *die* when his lips graze my neck, when his hand flattens on my belly and slides gradually down.

I've wanted this for *so long*.

A raucous peel of laughter rises from the tent. All at once, I'm back in my body, back in the present moment. All at once, I realize with painful clarity that Ben's hands are on me. His mouth is on me. I could let this happen, damn the consequences, damn the inevitable pain when it doesn't work out. When, God forbid, something happens to him.

Because it's dark, and it's late, and I've had too much wine, the thought comes to me: Andrews. Andrews, slipping off with my mother in the dark. Andrews, disappearing, alone in the forest. Andrews, the way my mother found her.

There's a dark well calling for me, and I'm sprinting toward it.

I pull away abruptly, turning to face Ben, a healthy few feet of distance between us.

"I'm sorry." The words spill, barely formed, from my mouth as I zip up my cargoes.

Ben takes a step back, looking stricken. "No, no, *I'm* sorry. Jesus, Jones. That was... that was out of line. Completely out of line. I didn't—"

"No, it's okay," I say quickly, knowing where his thoughts have gone. "I wanted to. I'm the one who..." The words catch in my throat. Am I about to cry? I shake my head. "Don't apologize. There's nothing to be sorry for. I just think this, our friendship, should stay professional."

He hesitates, then nods. Rubs the back of his neck with the hand that should be touching me. "Yeah. Of course. Absolutely."

I force a wan smile. "Cool. Okay. I'm heading to bed now."

"Right. Sleep well, Jones." He salutes me, turns on his heel, and strides away into the night.

Fuck. Fuck fuck fuck.

It takes everything in me not to go after him and bring him back here. It takes *everything* not to bring him back and throw him down on my cot and indulge in the most depraved acts I can think of.

Instead, pent-up and pissed off — at Ben, at myself, at Darcie and Julian — I retreat to my tent, undress, and crawl into my cot. There, I close my eyes and replay every second of what just happened over and over in my mind. Ben's breath on my hair, his hands on my bare skin, his hot mouth on my ear and neck.

It doesn't take long for me to come, but it's not satisfying. I lie there in the dark, breathing hard, trying and failing to hold back tears. I thought it would be easier out here.

That I'd be able to breathe for once, away from my own bullshit.

But here I am, the same Jill Jones as ever.

13

THE NEXT MORNING, Darcie and I decide to visit the forest. We've grown bored with the plain. Or Darcie has, complaining about its endless soft curves and the one tree Julian and Ben use as target practice, the tree they can't hit no matter how hard they try. I could spend a lifetime in those grasses, underneath this gorgeous sun.

The forest has been, up until now, Ben and Julian's domain. They're testing the air, looking for animal life, conducting all kinds of surveys. Darcie declares it's our turn that morning at breakfast, and I have no reason to argue. It doesn't matter that I'm still a ball of nervous energy, that my skin seems to hum from Ben's touch, even now. It doesn't matter that the forest makes the hair on the back of my neck stand on end.

Ben and I pointedly avoid eye contact in the main tent, despite him being an even brighter beacon to me now. He's a thing my body can't resist, pulling me in despite my best efforts.

"So, what's the deal?" Darcie asks when we're well away from camp.

"What deal?"

She glances sidelong. "Oh my God, you're so annoying when you're trying to play coy. With *Ben*, obviously. You were like a live wire in there just now, jolting whenever he came within five feet of you. And bitch, I saw him run after you last night. I'm not an idiot. Did you finally fuck?"

"No."

I turn to study Darcie's profile as we walk. There's something hard-edged in her tone, in the way the corners of her mouth are turned down. And then I see it. I was stupid not to notice. I've been so wrapped up in my blue balls to see anything past my own nose. Her eyes are shadowed, her brows drawn. And her movements are stiffer, more deliberate. The heavy cloud is back, enveloping her in its shadow.

"Too bad," she says.

She's not teasing me like she normally would. Suddenly, I don't want to go into the forest with her. Not when she's like this. I guess I naively thought the Planet was helping, that she was finally breaking free of the memories of her ex, his death, the trial.

Maybe we can't ever break free of things like that.

I button up my jacket to my chin. It's cold, and I'm glad I decided to wear my warmest wool socks.

We're nearing the tree line. It's an old, old forest. I can tell by the size and quiet of the trees, the way they seem to listen. I'll be able to calculate their ages with the proper equipment, but I know in my heart that they are ancient. Methuselah, Earth's oldest tree before it burned, was a child compared to these.

I allow myself to think about Earth, the broken thing we left behind. But instead of what it is, I think of how it was: our ancient biomes, the glorious balance of nature, the give and take. Plants consuming nutrients from the earth and sun; animals consuming plants; all of life, growing and decaying, and eventually giving itself to the soil. A perfect cycle, life and death playing out like poetry for billions of years.

Until we destroyed it.

"Darce," I say slowly. The trees rise up to meet us, and I'm dying to touch their rough bark. "Do you think we deserve it?"

She shoots me a look. "Deserve what?"

We come to the tree line, and I pause, lifting my palm to touch the closest tree trunk, its dew-wet bark. I close my eyes. "Hope. Saving. Another chance."

"Of course we do," she answers, her words glassy.

"We had our chance," I say, almost to myself, not caring if Darcie is interested in the conversation. "Our planet. We fucked it up. Maybe we shouldn't get a second one."

A hand falls on my shoulder. I open my eyes, and Darcie is staring at me with annoyance and a hint of something sharper. "The Planet is a gift. It's our opportunity to do it right this time. Now are you done having a moment? Let's go."

I hesitate.

I'm hyper-aware of her hand on me and my hand on the weathered bark of this ancient tree. But they're so utterly different. Each life, so incredibly varied, and yet... the same energy flows through us. The tree seems to sigh against me.

Oh, fuck.

Suddenly, I know exactly how old the tree is. I don't know how I know it, but I do. It has spent seven thousand eight hundred and thirty-nine years under this sun. Its lifeblood pulses deep, but I feel its relentless flow. *Hello*, I think, and I'm certain the tree understands. Darcie and I are conduits, electricity sparking through muscle and tissue, machines of biology, trillions of miles from home. The entirety of the forest is throbbing at such a deep, slow register that I shouldn't be able to sense it.

But I can.

The grass was one thing, its delicate touch, the way it soothed me, made me feel at home. But this is new. This is crazy. I can feel the forest's heartbeat. Or maybe I'm going insane.

"*Jill*," Darcie's voice cuts through my hazy thoughts. "You can touch as many trees as you want in your own time. Come on."

I draw my hand away from the trunk, following Darcie into the damp, cool forest. Soft moss seems to surge beneath my boots. Dripping ferns tentatively stroke my legs as I pass. The womb of the woods pulls us deeper in.

We should have come here sooner. I should have come here with Ben.

We drift deeper.

It's quiet. Like the vacuum of space, I think, an unplumbed depth. It's beautiful in the way of a Venus fly trap, or the deep melody of a black hole, unsettling but heady, intoxicating.

"What do you think?" Darcie says after a long, long silence. She gestures toward a cluster of white, round things thrust up from the soil in amongst the ferns. "Fungi? Could be interesting. The mycelium ecosystem would tell us a lot."

I nod, distracted. "Yeah. Good call."

She gives me a sour look. "Are you paying attention to anything I say?"

"What?"

"That's what I thought. What the hell is wrong with you, girl?"

I swallow, shaking my head. What *is* wrong with me? "I dunno. Sorry, Darce. It's the forest. I feel... weird."

She eyes me. "You look weird. Is it your mom?"

I'm immediately on the defensive. "What do you mean?"

"I *mean*, I can tell when you're thinking about her. So this forest must have some significance." Her voice takes on a patronizing tone. "It's okay if you don't want to go any further, you don't have to."

She's baiting me. I fucking hate it when she's like this. I know it's just a product of what she's suffered, but I'd rather not be on the receiving end of it. I wish we were back in the plain, wading in the icy river, laughing with the sky overhead. Now, all that's above us is thick boughs of interlocking leaves, green and brown and gray. If I was alone, or with Ben, I'd be fine. But with Darcie here...

"I'm fine," I say. I shouldn't let her get to me, but she does. "Let's grab the mushrooms and go. Unless you'd rather keep baiting me about my mom?"

Darcie shifts her weight, and for a moment, I think she'll turn away, focus on the mushrooms. Then a shadow passes over her face. "Don't you ever wonder if she did it?"

I'm actually impressed by the audacity. Of all the things I thought she'd ask, this wasn't at the top of the list, Dark Darcie or not. "If she *what*, murdered them?"

She shrugs. "They never did find the bodies."

"The deaths were never officially confirmed."

She eyes me, skeptical. "Like I said, they never found the *bodies*. But it's obvious."

There's something in Darcie's eyes that I don't trust. Is she still in control? Is she still Darcie at all? Because knowing what she did to her shitty ex, and being alone with her in the quiet forest with that expression on her face, are two entirely different things. I back away slightly. "What is?"

"Something went wrong." She tilts her head, hawk-like in the dusky light. "Someone went psycho and killed them all. Who else could it have been?"

"Fuck off, Darce." The words come out reedy and pathetic. Why did Darcie bring me out here? Why was she so insistent on visiting the forest? Unease flutters behind my ribcage. I suddenly wonder what this conversation would be like if Ben wasn't the only one with a sidearm.

"Andrews went first, didn't she?" Darcie persists. "Went into the forest, never came back."

I don't want to think about Andrews. "No, let's not—"

"There's a documented argument between her and your mother," Darcie continues, stepping toward me. "They almost came to blows."

"That's an exaggeration." Another weak protest.

Darcie makes a face. A face that says, *Don't kid yourself.*

"My mother wasn't like that," I bite out defiantly.

"I'm just saying." Darcie sniffs so casually that I suddenly want to lunge at her. "You know how it looks."

I hold her darkened gaze for a long moment. "Any more questions about how my mom is a killer?"

"That's all for now," she says.

And the way she says those four lazy words, like *I'm* the one who should bear the brunt of everything my mother saw and everything my mother lost, everything *I* never got to have, snaps something in me.

"No, go ahead," I press, angling toward her. "Keep going, Darce. Don't you want to know all the sordid details I *must* be holding back? Maybe you want some tips. Is that it? Hoping for some advice, killer to killer's daughter?"

At first, Darcie doesn't react. She only stares, her eyes so intense I take a step back. I shouldn't have said that. I really fucking should not have said that. I know she wouldn't hurt us, any of us, but the way she's looking at me now... well, maybe I'm not so sure. We're far from camp. She's taller and stronger than me. If I radioed Ben, if Darcie really wanted to, she could find some way to kill me before he got to us. We both know it.

After an interminable silence, she blinks. Rolls her neck. "Fuck you, Jill Jones."

"Fuck *you*," I throw back.

She narrows her eyes, then shrugs. "He deserved it."

I let out a slow, shaking breath. "I know."

"Murdering your abusive ex is inherently morally acceptable, you said."

"Well, that was..."

"You said."

"That was before you were being a dickhead."

She glares, and for a moment, the fear rushes back up my gullet, and I'm choking on it. This isn't Earth. We are trillions of miles from anywhere. Who would attend the funeral?

"I need more coffee," Darcie announces. "And I'm tired of looking at your pathetic, terrified face."

Before I can stop her, or apologize, or try to mend the rift between us in any way, she spins on her heel and strides away, back toward camp. Leaving me alone, utterly alone, deep in the forest.

14

I SHOULD GO WITH HER. If I don't, Ben will be pissed. And I don't want him to reprimand me, least of all because I'm afraid I might enjoy it. I should trail after Darcie like a kicked dog and hope to God she forgives me. Because that attack was well below the belt, and I knew it. My mom is one thing, but the shit Darcie went through... it's utterly another. I *know* what that asshole did to her. She's not a murderer. She defended herself. The judge agreed.

But the way she looked at me was terrifying. For the first time, I was afraid of her.

I find myself wandering deeper into the forest.

It isn't a conscious decision, but it feels like the right thing to do. Maybe it's Darcie's interrogation, but I feel close to my mother here. Like I can hear her voice in the faintly rustling leaves.

So I follow the memory of her, this woman who said she loved me so deeply but still couldn't make me into a whole person. There has always been something missing in me. She never allowed me to know my father, whoever he was. She never opened up to me. And so, here I am, seeking whatever she might give me with her memory, in this distant place where her life fell apart.

There are boulders and jutting bits of rock and earth all around now, the forest is getting harder to navigate the deeper I traverse.

I hear it before I see it, a low roar in the distance. A waterfall. It has to be.

Blessed with this new destination, I pick up my pace. And when I come around a moss-coated outcropping, there it is. Water plunges over the lip of drenched dark stone, frothy white, into an ice-cold stream below. I imagine glaciers feeding this waterfall, just like the river in the plain.

It's just a waterfall. It's just a forest. But I can't stop thinking about the fact that my mother was here once, standing right here, watching the same falls. It's *so* lovely. It looks like the sort of thing I'd cut out of an old history book as a kid, pinning to my wall, a shrine to incandescent beauty long past.

I breathe deeply, inhaling the thick air. It's different here than in the plain. The air is closer, almost palpable. There's a sense of unreality. The rush of water the only sound.

I needed this — to be alone, away from the others. I don't want to admit it to myself, but each of Darcie's questions felt like a knife between the shoulder blades. My mother wouldn't have hurt anyone. Couldn't have. Especially not Andrews.

I puff out a frustrated breath.

I can't let Darcie get to me. I'm just going to sit here and enjoy the waterfall, take some samples, and head back to camp. If I'm lucky, I'll make it back in time for lunch.

I settle myself on a moss-covered rock and watch.

The fall cascades down from a stone outcropping, around which the forest climbs upward toward snowy peaks. Our camp is at the foot of the mountains, their slopes purple-pale against the sky, but I can't see them now through the trees.

I think I could climb up there, to the top of the falls. There are uneven indentations, waterlogged ledges that might serve as makeshift steps. I see myself standing, moving to the rising land, the falling water. I see myself there, becoming part of the ragged landscape with every step, every press of skin against rock and water and moss, every footfall over lichen and slate.

A shiver runs up my spine.

The flutter of leaves catches my eye. I reach for a nearby fern, entranced by its beauty. Goosebumps rise on my skin, and warmth pools in my belly. I hold my palm out and upward, so the leaf lies gently flat for me to inspect. This isn't a species of fern I'm familiar with — of course it isn't — but it looks similar enough to Earth's ancient ferns that I'm a little taken aback. Everything here is similar to Earth. It's as if someone made a carbon copy of our planet and posted it up somewhere far away, with unnoticed differentiations.

I scan the fern with a critical eye and notice something strange. Strange, but exquisite. There are no imperfections here. No rips or holes from insects, no missing fronds, no pockmarks. It is exactly symmetrical. Every aspect of the fern is utterly pristine. I reach for another frond, delicately spreading it across my palm. It's the same. This is a perfect, impossible thing.

As I run my finger along the leaf, the hairs on my arm rise. The warmth in my belly burns hot, clenching at my core. I gasp at the sudden pleasure.

Jesus, am I aroused by a flawless example of botanical excellence? No, it's something else. Something more. I'm not thinking about sex. I didn't *mean* to feel that way.

Standing, I leave the fern and move to the nearest tree. Its trunk is thick, strong, and silvery. Its leaves hang long and tangled, silver-green in the shady wood. Will this tree, too, be perfect?

Delicate, almost hesitant, I lay my palm on the cool bark. I can feel the tree's life pulsing beneath my skin. The bark is smooth, but when I run a finger along it, I find that there are raised striations, and as I caress the tree so slowly... that latent pleasure unfurls inside me.

What does it mean?

I press my other hand to the tree. I study the bark closely. I don't know trees as well as I do their smaller cousins, but I do know that this is another perfect specimen. The almost invisible grooves in its trunk are regular, repeated, as if built by some cosmic hand.

It's stunning. I'm overwhelmed by it, this place. The grass must be the same. And the flowers that bloom in bursts throughout the plain. Biology doesn't work like this, it simply doesn't. At least, not on Earth.

I run my fingers down the tree's silvery trunk.

God. I arch my back at the sudden rush of sensation. My nipples peak. My breath grows shallow.

A twig snaps behind me.

I imagine his breath, a warm shiver across my exposed neck. I imagine drawing him into me, letting him touch me like I caressed the tree, the fern. I *know* it's him. I can hear him breathing. I feel his footfalls. The brush of his knuckles against the waving ferns.

I turn.

"Jones, what the hell are you doing out here alone?"

Ben's exasperation is on full display, and just for me. His chest rises and falls, his breathing just as shallow as mine. He hurried to get here. Maybe even ran.

"Sorry." I don't mean it. Not really. I like him coming here to retrieve me. I like him angry with me.

"Sorry? That's all?" He rubs a hand down his face. "Jones, learn to pick up your radio for once. I was worried."

My heart threatens to crack open and spill. "You were?"

He takes a step toward me. "Yes, I was."

The forest pulses through me, my skin tingling with its need. "Why?"

Ben comes up to me, crowds into my space, and reaches for my walkie. He makes a sound of deep disapproval, and there's a crackle from the device. Glaring at me through a spray of lashes, he presses on his own radio. "You turned off your goddamn walkie," he growls.

You turned off your goddamn walkie.

His voice, doubled, a split second delayed, rumbles from my own device.

He's still incredibly close. Is he thinking about last night? I am.

"I forgot." I haven't thought about my walkie at all, frankly. I've been distracted.

"I know I'm not your superior officer," he says, "but you can't just disregard the rules I put in place for safety reasons." He hasn't made a move to create space between us, and neither will I. His voice is low, gruff. His gaze flickers down, infinitesimally, to my mouth.

I remember his fingers deftly unzipping my pants.

"You're right, you're *not* my superior officer."

The forest wraps languid arms around me, the sensual rise of pollen from a jostled bloom, the delicate touch of a leaf against skin, the stolid trees throbbing with eager life. Breaths fill heavy lungs.

"But you *are* under my protection." Ben angles toward me, almost imperceptibly, his body warming me with its proximity.

"Protection from what?" Can he feel it? The gasp of this place, the indrawn breath and sultry moan? The prickling skin and the heightened senses? Distantly, almost with a sense of disbelief, I realize I've never been so turned on. Last night was nothing compared to this. I'm a powder keg rigged to blow. If he so much as looks at me a certain way, I'll—

"This place," he answers. His eyes are on my lips again. "The Planet."

I feel wholly detached from my body, and yet, every part of me is aflame, and I'm acutely aware of it. I'm not like this. I don't come onto people when I'm sober, when I'm working. Let alone Ben, who agreed we should keep this professional.

I lift my chin. "I don't need your protection."

He eyes me hazily, like he's drunk on this too. And he's still so close to me, intimately so. He hasn't moved away, hasn't put a workplace-appropriate distance between us. His jaw muscle tenses. "I'm the one who decides that. Just... don't be reckless."

What if you need protecting from me? I think nonsensically. But he wouldn't. He doesn't. I want him in the purest way, all of him, given to me freely.

I realize I can sense a fern as it curves over his boot, caressing his ankle. I suck in a sharp breath. The fern's leaves vibrate with want, asking *him* to explore the forest. Skin to skin. The forest is a quivering, desirous thing. I want him so badly.

He meets my gaze, disarmed, questioning but open. Trusting. Like he sees what I want, and he'll let me have it. His boot scrapes against an exposed root as he shifts his weight. He's warm and solid, and I want him, and the Planet wants him, and I've run out of reasons to say no.

Don't be reckless.

Too late.

I grab him by the collar. I lift myself up to my toes. He was already there, inches away. Our noses brush. I sigh, a soft exhalation of relief, and brush my lips to his.

There is a frozen hush. As if every leaf and frond and branch, the waterfall, the wind itself, has inhaled and held their breath.

Ben is warm and solid and rough; his lightly stubbled jaw against my skin sends a fresh shock of desire to my core.

I hold him here, suddenly desperate, knowing he might bolt, might push me away, might change his mind.

It's not a kiss, it's a question. A halting, eager plea. My eyes are shut tight, my fingers white-knuckling in his collar, our lips pressed together in a chaste softness.

The forest exhales.

And Ben comes to life.

15

BEN RESPONDS to my kiss with heady greed.

It's like a switch has flipped, and he is all in now. Every hesitation gone, reluctance chucked to the wayside. He wants this as much as I do. I can feel it. He takes my head in his hands, thumbs pressed to the soft skin beneath my ears. He angles himself to deepen the kiss, and when I reach up to bury the fingers of one hand in his hair, he rewards me with a groan.

A languid rush of desire, of pleasure, engulfs me. The trees ache with me. God, his mouth on me.

I've wanted him for so long.

One by one, he turns off our vest cameras. Distantly, I wonder if I should protest — we're supposed to keep those running at all times, for safety reasons... but the thought dissipates as he fumbles for my walkie, turning it off, flicking his off too. And then, putting one hand against my waist, he pushes me firmly backward until I hit the tree, rough against my back. He arranges my body just so, his hands confident and unhurried but desperately needy. He unbuttons the collar of my jacket, unzips it.

All the while, his mouth is on mine. His tongue delves deep, and I respond, clutching his hair, his flexed biceps. He lifts his knee to brace between my legs. I grind down on his muscled thigh and gasp, an embarrassing little cry spilling from my mouth.

His teeth clamp down on my lower lip as his hand slams against the tree trunk behind me. I feel his skin on the striated bark — I feel his hot skin on me — sparking, aching, about to *ignite*.

A wind picks up. The forest seems to awaken with it, rippling and gasping along with me.

"Do not," he says, muffled as he mouths my neck, "go out alone," he rips open my jacket, "ever again. That's an order."

I arch my back. From black damp soil, a seedling springs.

"Yes," I murmur.

Angling my hips, I move against him, desperate to gain purchase, the right angle for friction. He lowers his free hand, pressing his palm between my legs, giving me what I need.

"Yes, *what?*" he murmurs, his tone rich with praise and admonishment.

God.

"Yes, sir," I gasp.

"Good girl," he growls.

I'm writhing, dripping beneath him, falling apart by the seams. This is exactly what I wanted, but it's not enough. It's not enough.

Not enough, responds the forest. More seedlings burst from the soil, their leaves unfurling.

His hand moves, leaving me bereft, and I make a sound of protest. But it's only for a moment. He slides his hand under my jacket, brushing his fingers softly against my t-shirt. He moves his palm over my belly, curving his fingers around my side. Brushing upward with his thumb, he grazes the underside of my breast.

"Ben," I gasp. I'm losing my mind; I have never been so wound up. I'm aching, almost *begging* to get off. There's a tight, painful coil of want at my core, and I need him to give me everything. Unfurl me. Let me bloom.

From the seedlings explode a cacophony of blooms, painted bright and ecstatic. More and more, they grow. Vines trickle and coil down from above, encircling the tree. Encircling us, I imagine, pulling our bodies together until we're enfolded, part of the forest itself.

"Shh," he breathes. He sucks on my neck with practiced ferocity, as if he knows exactly how to make my heart stop with his mouth alone. How hard to bite before he leaves a mark. His hand roams deeper inside my jacket until his palm is flat against the small of my back. He pulls me close against him. He's firm, strong, military through and through. This is how he operates. I'm his mission.

"Please," I beg.

His hand slides down the tree bark, rough. Stars explode in my vision, a sharp, angry pleasure knifing through me. Yes. Touch me there. Anywhere. Run your fingers along a billowing fern. Sink into the earth, up to your ankles. Up to your knees. Let the Planet take you slowly, like a lover. Let her kiss the flesh from you. Sink in with me. Decay with me. Become bones with me.

"Please, *what*?" he says, and lowers his mouth to my breast, hot and wet at my skin-tight shirt, his tongue laving as he works me into the worst, most hedonistic frenzy. I feel unmoored. Uncontrollable.

I would be happy if we died here, like this.

"Fuck me," I gasp.

His muffled chuckle vibrates from my breast to my core, and I am so, *so* wet.

"Jones," he breathes, and then bites my nipple, hard.

"Ben, fucking *do it*." I'm ravenous.

A beat. The forest holds her breath.

Ben stops kissing me.

There's a sudden emptiness where he should be. I open my eyes, my head beginning to clear in his absence. He's no more than a foot away, but it feels like miles. His eyes are dark with lust, his hair an absolute mess, and God if I wouldn't do anything to have him all for my own, forever.

"You were right last night," he says, like it takes every bit of his strength to say it. "We shouldn't be doing this."

No, no, no. We *should*. Maybe he doesn't want to mislead me. He thinks I'll get too attached. "It's nothing," I gasp, hurried and wanting. "This thing between us, it doesn't have to mean anything. We can keep it casual. I won't let it affect my work."

He shakes his head, but I must sound so pathetic, so desperate, that he comes to me again. He presses his body to mine. He leans down, his head against my chest, and nuzzles my breast, murmuring my name. I whimper, grabbing at his hair, rolling my hips against his. I can *feel* his hard-on. He's probably leaking in his pants. He's right on the edge, just like me.

Stay here, Ben.

Again, he gently unfolds himself from me. Deliberately, slowly, like it takes everything in him to reject me for a second time.

"No," I demand, pulling him back to me with a hand hooked around his neck. "Come back. Just this once. We'll stay professional. It won't make a difference at all."

His gaze finally falls to mine. His pupils dilate, and for a moment, I think he'll change his mind. Yes. Come back to me, come into me. Let me swallow you.

I kiss him before he can protest, a hard, desperate, toothy meeting of mouths. He grunts, and I *will* him to stay. Stay. With me. In the forest. We never have to leave.

But he's stronger than me, and it doesn't take much for him to gently pry me away. He shakes his head, a wordless finality in his still-lustful gaze: We can't do this. *He* can't. He's military through and through. A consummate professional. And whatever just happened here...

"Jill Jones," he says, almost as if to himself. "Come on. Let's go."

Like flame deprived of oxygen, my arousal dissipates, scattering in the wind like ashes.

I lean back against the tree in my soaked underwear and saliva-wet shirt, and all I feel is shame. I threw myself at Ben in a moment of delusion. What the fuck was I thinking?

"You ready?" His expression is soft, and I hate that he's so kind, even when I've made an idiot of myself.

I nod. "Yeah, I'm right behind you. I just need a second."

His mouth tightens. He looks away. "Don't dawdle. Catch up to me, okay?"

"Okay."

He turns and strides off through the forest, back toward camp. As he fades into the dappled shadows, I hear a crackle as he turns his walkie-talkie back on. And I think I hear, before he disappears completely, "...won't make a difference to *you*."

Fuck.

I'll join him in a second. I just need a second.

I zip up my jacket, buttoning the collar around my neck as high as it will go. I smooth my hair and breathe out a long, self-loathing sigh. At last, I push away from the tree, ready to trail after Ben.

That's when I see it.

I thought I had imagined it. All around me are flowers. A mosaic. An undulating burst of riotous color — blooms I've never seen before. They form a bright circle around the tree where Ben almost made me come. I look and see vines looping down from its boughs. Countless thick, leafy vines that I swear weren't there before. And each leaf is perfectly symmetrical. Every flower petal is flawless.

The sight fills me with awe and unbridled fascination. What does it mean? Where did all of this come from? Was it attracted by something, by our activity? I need to understand. I should be taking notes, photographs, collecting samples.

But as I pause here, frozen amongst the inexplicable blooms, a prickle of fear invades my senses. My stomach curdles with dread. Andrews was here, deep in this forest. Alone. I don't know exactly what my mother saw when she found Andrews, but whatever it was, it broke her.

I don't want to take samples. I don't want to touch any of this. What if I, like Andrews, never make it out of the forest?

I take one last long look at the strange scene, the flowering mass, the moss and ferns, the waterfall that plunges beyond. Then I turn on my heel and run.

16

I CATCH up to Ben easily. And by the time we return to camp, the air between us is crackling with unspent tension. We hardly spoke on the walk, and I'm thankful for it. There's too much in my head, the flowers, the argument with Darcie — too much. And the last thing I want is to argue with Ben. So I keep my mouth shut.

But as we enter camp, it becomes immediately clear that something's wrong. A heavy, unseen cloud hangs over camp, vibrating at my senses, pressing down until my ears pop. Wrongness infiltrates every pore. Raised voices come from inside the main tent. Darcie sounds sharp and agitated. But Julian... Their voice cuts through me, even from the edges of camp. They're frightened. No, not just that. Terrified. *Different*. Like they've lost some part of themselves, and they're going mad.

I know a broken person when I hear one.

Ben and I share a look, then break into a run. We burst inside, shoulder to shoulder.

"Well, look who it is," Darcie spits, turning to us. "Tweedle Ho and Tweedle Slut."

Julian stares as if they hardly recognize us. They're sitting at the table, a cup of seemingly untouched water in front of them. Their glasses, folded neatly, sit next to the water. Their hair, usually pristine, is matted with dirt and bits of plant matter.

"What's going on here?" Ben demands.

Darcie snorts. "Like *you* care."

"He cares," Julian says, their voice devoid of inflection. They peer at Ben as if seeing him for the first time. "He's not our dad, but he cares like he is."

"Yeah, okay," Darcie says gently. "Whatever you say, Jules." I notice that her hands are shaking.

"Cut the bullshit," Ben barks. "Report. Now."

Julian flinches.

Darcie's nostrils flare. She lifts her chin, and I wonder how much fear is contained within her, how much she's trying to hide. "Something happened to Julian in the plain."

"No, no, I'm fine," Julian mumbles.

I can't take my eyes away from Julian. They're somewhere far away. This isn't the Julian I know.

"Explain," Ben says, jaw tight.

"After I came back to camp, right after you ran off after Jill for the millionth time," Darcie says acidly, "Julian wanted to go, I don't know, look at the grass or something."

"The tree," Julian says.

"Whatever, they wanted to check out the tree. The one you use for target practice. See if they made any bullseyes, I guess. I didn't want to. I said we could go later." Darcie's mouth twists. "They went anyway, without me. I didn't notice they were gone for ages, and then... well, by then it was too late."

Ben looks between Darcie and Julian, frowning. "Too late for what, Farreira? Is this a quarantine situation? 'Cause Fleming is not looking so good."

"I'm *fine*," Julian says, smiling distantly.

"Fuck off with your quarantine," Darcie snaps. "You think I'd be in here with them if I was worried about that? They're not *sick*. You didn't see— you didn't see what—"

"It's okay," Ben says, moving toward Darcie, hands up like he's attempting to calm a wild animal. "What did you see? Is there reason to believe there's an imminent threat here?"

Darcie scoffs. "Imminent? It already happened. You missed it."

Ben doesn't back down. "Is *Fleming* a threat?"

"I'm not a threat," Julian warbles. Their heavy-lidded gaze flits between Darcie and Ben.

"I know you're not," murmurs Darcie.

"We don't know that," Ben says at the same time. "I'd put you under quarantine, Fleming, but if there's something infecting you, it's probably infected all of us by now."

"That's kind of you," Julian mumbles. "But I'm okay. I think you should just let me go back. I didn't get to see all of her. There's so much of her. Like a painting. Like a painting. So perfect. I want to see all of her. So beautiful." Their words become chant-like.

Ben and Darcie share a hostile, loaded look.

"Jules, what happened?" I say, moving closer. Their

words spark a fear in me that I can't tamp down. "What did you see?"

Darcie eyes me with fiery disapproval.

Ben watches me too, tight-lipped. I wonder if he's worried I'll tell on us both. Or maybe he's regretting what happened in the forest.

"Jules?" I persist. "You okay?"

They nod, now staring sullenly at their water glass. "She kidnapped me."

I glance at Darcie. Raise my eyebrows.

"Nobody kidnapped anybody," Darcie growls. "Jules didn't want to come back to camp with me. I had to drag them. They were..." She throws up her hands, sighing. "It's impossible to describe. You won't fucking believe me."

"Yes, they will," Julian says, perking up. "She was so beautiful."

"Who was?" I ask, sitting next to Julian at the table. I'm so completely uninterested in what anyone else has to say.

"Fleming is obviously delirious," Ben says, almost a warning.

"Shut *up*," Darcie barks.

"Jules," I press. I lay a hand on their shoulder, and they jerk slightly, as if they hadn't realized I was there. "It's okay. You can tell me, I believe you. Who did you see in the plain? Who was so beautiful?"

They turn to me, their dark eyes glazed with faraway tears. Their cheeks are flushed red, feverish in the lamp-light. "The Planet."

Ben shifts his weight. I notice his hand rests on his gun.

Darcie crosses her arms.

"The Planet?" I repeat. "But she's everywhere."

"Yes," says Julian, lighting up. "She is. God, she's beautiful. I saw her out there, on the plain. She called to me. So, I went to her."

My heartbeat thuds heavily in my ears. The room narrows to just Julian and me. "What did she say to you?"

A tear falls from Julian's eye, running along their cheek until it disappears beneath their chin. Their voice is a low hush, their lips quivering. "That everything's going to be okay."

"That's all?"

Julian blinks. "No, that's not *all*. She showed me the most beautiful thing. Like a dream, you know, so vivid, better than Earth. Better than anything. It was so perfect. So beautiful. Like a painting."

"A painting of what?"

Julian's brows furrow. They shake their head. "It was so perfect. I just wanted to see more. To be happy. But Darcie kidnapped me. She won't let me go back. Jill?"

"Jules?"

They hold my gaze with a watery stare. Their pupils are enormous black pools, so dilated that I see no iris at all. "She interrupted me. Bring me back, Jill?"

"I..."

"See?" Darcie says, and my surroundings come rushing back. "They're traumatized. This is your fault."

"They're sick," Ben corrects.

"No, they're fucking *not*," Darcie spits, her eyes wide with rage. "Fuck you. I saw something insane out there. It was... it was the grass, and flowers, and—"

"Darcie," I interrupt, swallowing a bead of fear, "did you have your vest cam on?"

There's a moment of tense silence. I wonder if Darcie is thinking the same thing I am: That she could demand to see our cams, see what happened between Ben and me in the forest. That she'd get nothing out of it because my cam is still off. I hold my breath.

"Yeah," Darcie says, "yeah. I did."

My relief is short-lived. We sit around the table and set up Ben's tablet, using an empty mug as a tripod. No one speaks. I could cut the tension with a knife. We crowd around as Ben transfers the mini tape from Darcie's cam to his tablet. Even Julian seems mildly interested, their attention drifting from the middle distance to the screen as Ben fast-forwards to the right time stamp.

The vid begins.

The footage is grainy and dark, but I recognize it immediately as the plain. Grasses arc toward Darcie as she walks, reaching for her. But that's not what I focus on. My gaze is drawn immediately to a strange shape in the distance, rising above the grass. Something almost human, but too tall, writhing and blurry.

"What the...?" Darcie's voice comes through warped in the recording. "What the fuck is..." There's a crackle: her walkie. "Ben, come in."

Nothing.

"Benjamin, *respond*." Panic rises in her voice. Crackle. "Jill? Come in."

Silence.

My stomach turns to stone, and I feel Ben pointedly *not* looking at me.

"Where the fuck *are* you, assholes?"

Then Darcie starts to run. The camera shakes violently as she sprints forward, and the distant shape grows clearer.

"Jules," Darcie calls out, strangled. "Jules! Jules?"

I can't make it out. I can't see what she sees.

Darcie stops suddenly and bends over, the camera fixed on her boots in the grass. She's breathing hard, winded from the run. "Fuck," she repeats.

When she straightens, we finally see it. A human shape. Julian. It can't be anyone but Julian, though their silhouette is dark against the sky in the grainy video.

"What is that?" Ben asks, peering at the screen.

"Shut up and watch," Darcie snaps.

I shoot a furtive look at Ben, and like an idiot, he's already watching me. I press my lips together and turn back to the tablet. I don't want it to be true, but I know what I see. It's not just Julian in the video. It's Julian and a thick, writhing column of vines. The vines encase Julian's form, lifting them up until they're at least eight feet tall, their feet dangling, their head thrown back as if in agony. Or ecstasy.

The vines sway, holding Julian aloft. They slowly coil around their limbs like snakes, tighter and tighter.

"Jules," Darcie says in the video like a hopeless prayer, and there is a rip of Velcro and the sound of fumbling. She's looking for something in one of her pockets. The video becomes obscured by her hands for a moment. "Where is it?" she whispers desperately. "*Where is it?*"

But I'm focused on what's happening to Julian in the vid. Flowers begin to sprout from the vines, and like a time-lapse, they bloom all at the same time. Loud, spring-like, vibrant flowers. Just like the ones in the forest.

Julian begins to shudder on screen.

I feel sick. I think of my mother, her team disappearing one by one. Did they... was this... is this what happened to *them*? But I don't even know what *this* is.

I'm going to throw up.

Somehow sensing my discomfort, Ben reaches out a hand, hooking my pinky finger with his. The small gesture grounds me. Brings me back in the present.

In Darcie's video, Julian falls still. Their head lolls. And from their mouth, delicate and triumphant, blooms a white flower.

The camera shakes. Darcie rushes forward, uttering a string of curses. She's hacking at the vines with a knife, hacking and hacking, pulling with her free hand. The vines break and snap, and with each severed strand, they fall to the ground.

"We don't have to keep watching," Darcie says, her voice dull. "I obviously cut them free. They survive."

"Wait," I say, eyes glued to the recording. "I need to—"

Ben reaches over and switches it off. There's a crackle, and the screen goes dark.

"Ben," I protest, throwing him a look. I need to see what happens.

He shakes his head.

Darcie grits her teeth.

"See? Darcie kidnapped me," Julian murmurs. "You saw it. I was safe. Everything was perfect. Beautiful. Like a painting."

Darcie says, without inflection, "I pulled that flower out of Julian's mouth. An entire root system came with it. They were puking blood afterward. It *grew out of them*."

"That's impossible," I say automatically, snapping into scientist mode, a coping mechanism. "Plants can't—"

"No, you're right, Jill," Darcie interrupts, spinning on me. Her eyes are black with rage. "I doctored the footage. I did it all for a laugh. Did you enjoy my prank, you fucking pedantic botanist bitch?"

"Farreira, that's enough." Ben's tone falls heavy over the group. "No one's saying you lied. It's just a hell of a lot to take in."

"Of course you'd defend her," Darcie snipes. "You've been mooning over her since day one."

Ben and I glance at each other, then turn away as if burned. He hasn't. Darcie's just angry, winding us up.

"Don't be mad," Julian says, turning to Darcie. "I know you were trying to help. But it's okay. Next time, you don't have to."

Darcie's nostrils flare, her jaw taut. For a moment, she sits there, saying nothing. Abruptly, she stands, gives us all an icy glare, and storms to the exit. When she reaches the tent flap, she turns.

"Next time," she says, catching and holding my gaze, "at least keep your walkies *on* while you're fucking in the woods."

17

DUSK BEGINS to fall over camp. Darcie's gone off alone. I feel choked with fear for her, unable to focus, unable to calm myself. Why would she wander off like that, after she saw what happened to Julian? Ben insists she'll come back, she just needs space. For some reason, the video hasn't shaken him like it has me. Maybe he's seen worse in war, or maybe he's too stubborn to let it truly sink in — that Julian was encased in writhing vines, that they were lifted up, nearly *consumed*.

I know one of us — probably Ben — should go after Darcie, bring her back. But the last thing I want is to lose him.

"Darcie's okay," Julian says dreamily from their bunk. Their arms are wrapped around their legs, knees tucked under their chin.

Ben and I have been taking turns checking in on Julian throughout the day. They're not getting any better. If anything, their eyes seem even more faraway than this morning, their words less and less cogent.

"Why do you say that?" I ask, not expecting a meaningful answer. I've made myself comfortable in a chair I dragged in from the main tent and brought in a mug of cold coffee to sip.

"Because we all are," Julian answers.

I glance up from my coffee. "What do you mean?" It's been this, over and over. We're all okay, everything is fine, perfect. Darcie stole Julian away from some eternal ecstasy, and so on. Pure madness. I don't know what Julian experienced in the plain, but it wasn't beauty. All I saw in that video was abomination.

A line forms between Julian's brows. "I mean the Planet loves us."

I roll my shoulders to dispel an impending shudder. "Planets don't have feelings."

"This one does."

A chill runs up my spine. I think of the legend of Gaia, the goddess of Earth, birthing strange beings into a quiet world. But we are far from Earth. Gaia doesn't exist here. She doesn't exist anywhere. There's nothing but rock and flora, and far below us, a boiling white-hot core at the center of this celestial body. Just like every other goddamn planet in the universe.

I try to swallow the knot of dread that's caught in my throat. Even logic and science do nothing to soothe me just now.

"You should get some sleep," I say, standing. I suddenly don't want to be in here with Julian. Their eyes are too hazy, their bizarre words too earnest. I need familiarity, comfort, before I get pulled in and start to drown alongside Julian.

"I'm not tired," Julian protests. "I close my eyes and see Her."

"Great," I say, distracted and wound up. I turn to go.

"Wait."

I pause and look over my shoulder. Julian's watching me intently. "I thought you understood," they murmur.

I don't want to know. I don't want to know. I ask: "Understood what?"

"Your mother. I thought you knew."

I take a step back. The mug falls from my fingers, and cold brown liquid splashes my boots. "Knew what?"

But they only smile, a painfully slow expansion of the lips. "Never mind. I thought you knew. You'll find out soon."

I back out of the tent, spin on my heel, and run. I can't catch my breath. Can't get away fast enough. I sprint across the camp, ready to collapse the second I get to my tent.

I'm just a meter away when a shape darts out of the shadowy dusk, slamming into my side. I stumble, nearly losing my balance. Before I can regain composure, an arm clamps around me, pulling back against my throat. My attacker is breathless behind me, their exhalations hot on my ear.

"Bitch," Darcie hisses.

I try to speak, but her arm is pinned against my windpipe, and I can't force out the words. I can't breathe. I kick at her, pulling at her arm, already panicking. But she's taller than me, far stronger, and extremely pissed off.

"That sucks, doesn't it?" she murmurs in my ear. There's an oiliness to her tone that I've never heard before. "Not being able to breathe. No way to fight back."

Fuck. I'm going to die here. Pathetically, helplessly, in Darcie's arms. I wonder distantly if I deserve it. Somewhere, deep inside, I think I do. My struggles weaken.

"Imagine how Julian must have felt," Darcie continues, her crushing grip on my neck tightening further. My vision spots. "The grass, the flowers, the very ground they walk on, all using them as glorified fertilizer."

Her voice seems to come from far away. Through water, a thick fog. There's no use fighting anymore.

"All because you couldn't keep it in your pants. All because Ben was so desperate to get his dick wet."

Ben.

His name wakes me and pushes me back toward consciousness, even though I know my weakening kicks against her shins, my scrabbling fingers at her arm, aren't going to save me. Darcie's going to come for him next. When I'm gone, she'll hunt him down. She'll use his gun to shoot him, or she'll bait him into shooting her first. Either way, I won't be the last to die.

"Shh," Darcie purrs. "Only a moment now." Her mouth brushes my ear, and I'm disgusted. I want to rip her head off with my bare hands and crush it under my heel. I want the Planet to devour her, grow inside her, replace her intestines with vines, her veins with root systems. I want her opened-up body dripping with blood and sap, consumed, decimated.

My panic dissipates.

All around me, darkness. I'm relaxing into it. My body is going limp. Falling asleep.

Darcie, comes a voice — my own thoughts, from deep,

deep inside. *Let me go. It doesn't have to be like this. Let me go, and She'll spare you.*

A hiss of indrawn breath. A curse spat in my ear.

And then I'm on my knees in the dirt, choking and coughing, tears streaming down my face. I vomit, still half-blind. I can see enough now to know that Darcie's gone. I'm alone in the night. She couldn't have been here longer than a minute, maybe two. Cricket-things chirp all around the camp. The stars watch impassively from above.

Darcie tried to kill me.

The thought runs through my head like a marquee. Darcie tried to *kill* me. Or she wanted to scare me so badly that I'd never... never what? Turn off my walkie again? Piss her off? Make out with Ben?

Fuck. She's out there now, wandering in the darkness. I stand, hobble to my tent, and crawl onto the cot. My lungs and throat scream in pain every time I take a breath. Darcie saw something unthinkable out on the plain today. We all saw it, but not in the way she did. Not with the pure terror she did, with the fear of losing Julian.

I pulled that flower out of Julian's mouth. An entire root system came with it.

I retch over the side of my cot, but nothing comes up this time.

We're all acting insane. Is it the Planet? The fucking Napa wine?

"There's a biological explanation," I mutter to myself, twisting my fingers together. "There always is." But what about Julian's behavior? What about my own, the way I threw myself at Ben? Darcie choking me half to death?

Toxic air. Microspores that alter the mind. It could be anything. Something they missed in the first expedition.

I remember my conversation with Julian in the lab tent. We're all broken in some way. Damaged, maybe unfixable. No one would care if we disappeared out here, one by one. Maybe that's exactly what they expect to happen, as long as we find the results they want.

I don't know how long I sit on my cot in silence, gently massaging my throat, wishing I'd been stronger, that I had tried harder to stop Darcie. And I know I should call for Ben on the radio, tell him that no one is safe on their own. But I don't want to have to explain what Darcie did. It's my fault, I'm sure of it. My fault.

Julian's words pop into my head, unbidden: *I thought you knew... You'll find out soon.*

I don't fucking know, do I? I don't know *anything*. This place is a cruel joke. Maybe Julian is trying to hurt me. Why would they know anything about my mother that I don't?

"Knock, knock." Ben's voice outside the tent is soft, hesitant.

I start at the sound, my hackles rising. I'm wound so tight I'm about to snap.

"Come in." My voice is faint and weak.

He pushes aside the flap, ducks inside, and sits beside me. His hair is still slightly disheveled from our tryst in the forest, his collar drawn up, his jawline shadowed in the lantern light. He shouldn't be allowed to look like that when I feel like this.

I open my mouth to say something, to tell him what

happened. I have to tell him Darcie attacked me. But I know what he'll do next. He'll tell me to stay put, and he'll go looking for her. Anything could happen, after that.

"I just went to check on Fleming," Ben says. "They said you high-tailed it out of there a bit ago. You all right?"

Darcie tried to kill me, actually.

"No," I answer. "Not really." I turn to him, and I'm struck by the sweetness in his gaze. How can he be so soft, so kind, after everything? After what we saw happen to Julian? After what I made him do in the forest? Made *us* do?

"Yeah, I figured."

"I'm sorry," I say, my voice breaking. "I didn't mean— I just, I thought it was safe, and I didn't— It's my fault, I'm so sorry—"

"Shh," he murmurs, hooking an arm around me and pulling me into him. "Nothing's your fault. You haven't done anything wrong. No one's hurt. We're all okay."

"Julian's not okay." And I'm not okay. I'm extremely far from okay. But I can't speak the words. It's as if they're wrapped in stinging nettles, caught in my throat.

"They're just sick," says Ben. "They're running a temperature. I gave them something to lower the fever, and I'll check in later tonight."

His arm is still around me. I'm pressed to his side, and I allow my head to fall sideways until my cheek rests on his shoulder. I'm still taut as a wire, my heart hammering in my chest, skin prickling with fear, but Ben is solid and real and comforting.

"I know it's hard," he says, after a minute or two of

quiet. "Being here, knowing what your mom went through. But it's all gonna be fine, I promise."

I close my eyes. "How can you promise that?"

He turns, pressing an awkward kiss to my head. "I can't. But I've spent a while getting to know you. Maybe not as well as Fleming and Farreira do, but I know you well enough. I know you think you're defined by everything your mother did. That you have to fit into the shape of what she left behind. But you don't. You just have to be Jill."

With each word he speaks, my muscles relax, just a little. I don't dare open my eyes. If I do, he'll dissipate into mist, and this kindness, the care in his words, his gentle kiss, will all have been a dream.

"And Jones," he continues, "you're more than enough. You're a force. Smart. Pretty. Kinda quiet. Sarcastic." I can hear the smile in his voice. "Annoying, when you're in a mood."

Darcie's words ring in my ears: *You've been mooning over her since day one.* Have I been too oblivious to notice? Too caught up in hiding my own crush that I completely missed what was staring me in the face? All I needed was a pissed off, murderous Darcie to show it to me.

Fuck. Darcie.

I sit up and turn to Ben. I don't know how to ask him if he means it. I don't know how to explain that everything he believes about me is wrong. I don't think I *am* any more than my mother's daughter. No one ever allowed me to be. So instead of saying what I want to say — that I need him, I care about him, I want him to hold my hand and never let go — I clear my throat and say, "Did you see Darcie on the way here?"

He tucks a stray piece of hair behind my ear. "No. But I'm sure she'll be back. Just has to get something out of her system. If she's not back by midnight, I'll go look for her."

How can he be so *unbothered?* I don't know what to say next. I can't tell him what she tried to do, or he'll go looking for her. The last thing I want is for him to leave my side, even though part of me is desperate to make sure Darcie is safe. Part of me yearns to look after Julian.

But Ben... I can't help the way my body reacts to him. And that other part of me, the traitorous one, the louder one, is hungry for comfort. For another taste.

"What do you think that was?" Ben asks, his thoughts clearly miles away.

He doesn't have to say, *In the video.* I know what he means. I meet his gaze. There's fear in his eyes, and a little hope. Like he thinks I might have an answer, like maybe I'm the solution to everything in his life. It's intoxicating.

I take a breath before answering. *I don't know. An impossible thing. A nightmare.*

An evening breeze snakes in through the open tent flap, and with it, the smell of fresh blooms. The smell of grass, of rich soil, of dew-wet ferns. A flood of pleasure drenches me, washing me clean. Somehow, I know the dusk is turning clear and crisp, a purplish velvet paradise, and suddenly, all of this feels so small. So unimportant. I want to be outside, under the stars, amongst the grasses and trees and buds. All I want is to explore.

Everything else can wait.

Slowly I stand, holding out my hand.

Ben takes it, his expression curious. But I see the lust

there, simmering behind his eyes. I feel it, too. We're burning like embers.

I answer his question: "I'll show you."

18

BEN DOESN'T HESITATE. There's no worry in his gaze, no mistrust in the set of his shoulders or in the soft smile he gifts me. I lead him from the tent and into the darkening night. There is a line of rich purple on the horizon, the last vestige of day, but I am not afraid of the night. Not anymore, not when the scent of growing things is in the air. Not when the moons glow whitely in the blue-black sky, lighting our way.

We walk hand in hand, south into the plain. The grass is soft and cool, welcoming us with gentle touches.

"Where are we going?" Ben asks.

I say nothing. I can barely think over the ache of need in my core, the way I want his hands all over me. But not in a tent. Not inside.

I need him here, out here under the sky and among the grasses and the blooms.

When we're out of sight of camp, I stop and turn to face him. He's perfect in the moonlight, the planes of his face illuminated in pale blue. I glance down at his gun. His left hand rests there, loose and casual. Is it a habit, or doesn't he trust me?

"Ben," I murmur, lifting a hand to gently run my fingers down his front. His chest is firm, filling out his t-shirt so perfectly.

He smiles slowly, like something's falling into place. The hand on his gun relaxes, and he lets it fall to the side. "Jones. What is it you wanted to show me?"

The grasses bend to us like praying congregants. Like eager souls lined up to enter paradise. They touch me, reverent, and with every brush against my legs, a ripple of desire runs through me and clenches at my core. I have never needed anything like I need Ben right now.

But he's no longer looking at me. He's studying the grass. "So pretty," he says, extending a calloused hand to brush across the blades of green.

I shudder at the touch. It's like lightning straight to my inner thighs. I'm so turned on I might explode. I can't speak, or I'll moan his name.

"I'll never get over this," he says, now caressing the grass with both hands. He bends to look more closely. "How it follows my movements. Like it's saying hello."

I watch, wordless, enraptured. He extends a finger in the moonlight, running it up and down one of the silver-green blades of grass, slow and gentle. As he does, the grass shivers, curling toward his hot skin. All around him, the flora bends and reaches and aches to touch him. *I* ache to touch him. But I can't interrupt this.

"It's beautiful," he breathes. He looks out over the plain, up at the moon, then back to the undulating grass. He lets out a long breath. "God. It's so beautiful."

When he finally straightens and turns to look at me, my chest aches. His gaze is a reflecting pool of love, a depthless well of unconditional adoration. But is it for me, or the Planet?

"It's probably nothing to you, a genius botanist," he says, running a thoughtless hand over the grass. My skin heats. "You know, this Planet..."

I move closer, and he doesn't step away. I need him, but I don't want to frighten him away with my eagerness, not before I know he's mine.

"The Planet?" I prompt. I'm not afraid anymore. How could I be, out here, under the endless sky?

"It's different than I expected. I see why your mother spoke so highly of it, even though..." he swallows. "Sorry, I—"

"It's okay." Say it. Give yourself to me. I need you.

He shakes his head. "It's just that I've never seen something this beautiful." He's looking right at me when he says it. "Humanity's last hope. You know, I was nervous to come here, but..."

I lift a hand to cup his jaw.

He inhales sharply.

"But what?" I ask.

He leans down, his lips brushing mine. I feel his heartbeat through his shirt. "But it turns out I kinda love it."

There.

My fingers tangle in his hair and I drag his mouth to mine. I can't help the little moan that escapes me in the heated collision. I'm already soaking wet, desperate for more, but I'll let him take his time. I don't know what he wants from me, but I'm willing to give him everything.

Every inch. And by the time he's done, he'll be utterly mine. And I'll be his.

He kisses me rough and hard, like he needs to devour me now, right now. I feel exactly the same. His mouth is desperate on mine, his hands pulling me into him. I relish the press of my body to his, my breasts against his chest. Our legs interlock; hips perfectly aligned.

He takes hold of the back of my neck in one hand, holding me in place while he rolls his tongue inside my mouth. I swallow his groan, frantic with need. There are too many clothes. There is too much between us. I need his skin to meld with mine. I need him deep inside me. I need to become part of him.

As if reading my mind, he undoes my jacket, pushing at it until it falls from my shoulders and into the grass. Then he hooks his fingers under the hem of my shirt, lifting it up and over my head. "Fuck, Jones," he mumbles, licking and nuzzling my bare breasts with his mouth while fumbling at my belt. "You're so beautiful. I need to touch you. I have to feel you. I need to know how wet you are for me."

I bite the inside of my mouth. He finally gets my pants unzipped and shoves them down to my knees. He doesn't waste any time, sliding his hand between my legs, pressing his fingers to the underside of my panties. I can't help the way my hips jerk into his touch, just as he groans low in his throat.

"God, Jones, you *are* wet for me. You're soaking."

I respond by rolling my hips down onto his hand, greedy for friction. *Please. Give it to me. Give yourself to me.*

"Shh, shh," he murmurs sweetly, pushing my panties

aside with rough fingers. He slides one finger up and into me, curling it slowly at the knuckle, and I could scream at the sudden indescribable pressure. "Is that what you wanted?" he asks. Then, quietly, as if to himself, his finger working slowly in and out: "You're so tight. So fucking tight, Jones. I knew you'd be."

The plain ripples like a storm-torn sea. It's true night now. The line of purple on the horizon has faded and gone. There's nothing but moonlight and the blazing hot need at my core, this desperate ache for Ben, for all of him, until there's nothing left.

He slides another finger in to join the first, and I arch my back in white-hot pleasure. If he wasn't holding me up with his free arm, I would be gone. I would melt into the soil and rot, pushed to the edge of desire for eternity by the maggots and worms in my carcass.

"Jones," he orders. "Look at me."

I can't help but obey. I'll let him take the lead, let him march willingly into me until we're one, until we're both drowning deep where no one can save us. His gaze holds me with a warmth, a want, that I've never felt before except with Ben. I'll do anything he wants.

The grass undulates around us, dancing, whipped into a frenzy that mirrors ours. It strokes the backs of my thighs with feather-light touches. The coil of pleasure in my core grows to an impossible ache.

"I have been mooning over you," Ben rumbles, breathless, plunging a third finger deep inside me as I cling to him, my arms thrown around his neck, "since day one."

He kisses me like it's the last thing he'll do before he dies. It's a relentless, euphoric crash of lips and teeth. He pauses just long enough to say, "I wanted you before I even met you."

I feel like I'm floating. The grasses ripple around me, coiling at my thighs, reaching up, caressing me alongside Ben's fingers. And then his thumb brushes my clit, once — *fuck* — twice — *I'm so close* — and then he presses down, holding pressure there, his fingers still deep inside me, the grass stroking my hot skin, and I nearly lose it altogether.

"Wait," I gasp against him, pulling away.

The night goes cold for an instant. The grass recedes. Our gazes meet, and I realize what Ben thinks — that I changed my mind.

"I'm sorry," he rumbles. "Are you—"

"Shh," I say. "I want you inside me when I come."

His already lust-filled gaze darkens further. He engulfs me again, his mouth on my neck, my ear, nipping at my breasts. As if spurred by his action, the grass surges around me again, sweeping along my most intimate parts, and I groan in barely contained ecstasy.

I fumble at Ben's pants, the belt buckle clanking as I pull it free. I unzip his fly and pull down his briefs. His cock springs free, gorgeous, and brownish pink. He groans my name as I wrap a hand around his length, testing his girth. He's perfect. I look up and see that he's watching me, the want in his eyes incomprehensibly hot.

"Jones—" he groans.

I need him. I need him to fuck me. I need him inside me, filling me up. I want him dripping out of me, hot and thick. He's *mine*. Grasses reach for us, caressing us. Touching Ben in the ways I can't with only two hands. The gentle blades of green coil up against me, teasing my entrance, and I bite back a moan of pleasure.

This is how I'll have him. Here, in the plain, under the moons and the sky.

I kick off my boots and pants, and then Ben lowers me until I'm straddling him, naked and soaking. The plain pulses around our bodies, watching, participating. I lower myself over Ben's erection, the unspeakable sensation of his tip at my entrance, teasing. I'm taut and ready.

Down here, my knees in the dirt, it's all too easy for the grass to curve toward us, to gently stroke our skin. I feel soft pressure against my breasts, and I know it's the plain. The Planet.

I lower myself onto him slowly, so slowly. The slide of him inside me is so overwhelming. He fills me up so perfectly that I can't see, can't breathe, can't think.

Ben's thumbs brush my nipples, then his mouth, his teeth, and I throw my head back. My hair mingles with the green all around us. This is where I belong. I feel like I was born here, and I'll die here. He's nearly bottomed out inside me, our bodies moving together in perfect unison. My wet core tightens as our fucking grows frenzied. He licks my nipple, and I gasp.

The grass convulses all around us as my climax approaches.

Ben repeats my name like a prayer.

"Jones," like I'm a goddess.

"Jones," like I'm his world.

"You take me so well," he praises as my ecstasy begins to crest. "You're so good," he breathes, and everything at my core begins to tighten in all-consuming pleasure. "So perfect. So perfect."

All of my pleasure, my pent-up want, this ache I've borne for Ben for over a year, tightens to a singularity. My vision blacks out.

Darcie bathes in the moonlight. She's at the edge of a shallow river, up to her hips in the water. Silver-blue light glints off the slow drift of the river's current. She's completely naked, her breasts heavy with desire. Her eyes are closed, one hand rolling a nipple between two fingers, the other in the water, down between her legs.

Her breaths are shallow. Short, sharp gasps fall from between her full lips. She bites down on her lower lip, like the pleasure is too much. Like it might drown her.

"Yes," I gasp, and I feel Ben and the Planet inside me, beneath me, all around me. Ben is close, too. So close.

Darcie. Come with us.

Darcie lets out a long, breathy moan, just as I lose control. I'm rising with the headiest pleasure I've ever felt, an orgasm that spans between souls, between stars.

As I ride the wave, Darcie disappears beneath the water.

I'm crying out, and I don't know whose name I'm gasping. Ben's, Darcie's, or something else entirely. I'm under the water with Darcie. I'm in the river, rolling my hips. Ben is deep, deep inside me, just about to come, his hands gripping my hips, guiding me, holding me there at the apex of perfect pleasure.

Darcie's back arches as she sinks to the riverbed, her hand still between her legs.

I scream, undone, overwhelmed, *on fire*, as Darcie sinks

into the mud. As she, too, screams, her face a twisted rapture. Down, down, her body descends as if the ground is opening up to take her into its womb, a birth reversed.

As she disappears below the mud, her expression is the purest bliss.

I shudder as the last of my orgasm rolls through me. And when I open my eyes, Ben is crying out, digging bruises into my hips with his fingers as he fills me, overflowing. The plain waves all around us, brushing us with want, and my skin is on fire.

I want Ben like this, always.

After a time, the world fades into focus.

My face is buried in the crook of Ben's neck, his pulse still racing. He smells like sweat and soil. The back of my neck prickles. I sit up, still straddling him, his cock still deep inside me. I splay a hand on his chest to hold myself steady, sucking in a breath.

"Ben," I murmur.

"Mmm?" he mumbles, still blissed out on sex, still hard. He reaches up as if to touch my jaw with languid fingers and pauses. His gaze looks past me, to the grass all around us.

Only it's not just grass. It's a blaze of moonlit flowers.

19

BEN REACHES out to touch one of the blooms. Hypnotized, I watch as his fingertip brushes the delicate edges of night-pale petals. Slowly, almost hesitant, as if worried he might bolt, the flower coils around his finger, its stem elongating like a tendrilous vine. More flowers join it, a bouquet encircling his fingers until his entire hand is covered in blooms.

A thought comes to me from far, far away: *This is what happened to Julian.*

Do something, Jill.

But I can't. I, too, am enraptured. My skin buzzes, my nipples harden. Desire drenches me again, and I can't help it.

"Are you seeing this?" Ben breathes, and I realize distantly that he's not afraid. He's in awe. "The flowers. They're so beautiful. Perfect. Like a painting."

The words snap me back to reality. Everything sharpens.

"No," I blurt, clambering off Ben and scrambling to my

feet, pulling at the flowers. Still-warm cum drips down my inner thigh. "Don't *touch* him." I crush soft petals in my hands, ripping at the stems, frantic, until Ben's hand is free.

I stand there, shaking, naked amongst the hateful blooms.

"Jones?" Ben says, still half-lying in the flower-scalded grass, raised up on his elbows.

"Get dressed," I order, trying to sound brave, my voice betraying me. "Now. And don't touch the flowers."

He frowns, opens his mouth as if to question, then changes his mind. He nods once and begins to pick himself up. I'm already half-dressed, my jacket gone in the thicket of flowers. I give it up for lost, shoving my feet into my boots, not bothering to lace them. As soon as Ben's feet are in his boots, his jacket hanging from one arm, I grab him by the hand and drag him back toward camp.

He follows, obedient, still sex-addled or something else. I'm afraid to know. My heart beats a staccato in my throat, and I refuse to think about what would have happened if I hadn't been there. If Ben had been alone in the grass.

Why did I bring us out here?

He stops me on the way to Julian's tent, squeezing my hand and pulling me back to him.

"Jones, what's going on?"

I stare up at him. "I need to make sure Julian's okay."

He shakes his head, blinking, gazing into the dark. "Those flowers... They came out of nowhere. It was—"

"If you say *perfect like a painting*, I'm going to shoot you with your own gun," I snap.

His expression turns serious. "Did I miss something?"

I grab him by the collar and pull him close, savoring his

warmth, his smell. He holds me with his gaze, sweet and sinful, like he wants to take care of me, like he wants to ravage me. His pupils are still a little dilated, a little too dark.

"Fuck," I hiss. Not him. Leave him alone. Why not *me* instead?

"What's wrong, Jones?" he asks, tucking my hair behind my ear. He leans in, kissing my ear. "So beautiful."

"Ben," I say, gritting out my words, trying to remain calm, sane, functional. "Do me a favor and get me some water? I'm gonna check on Julian."

"Right," says Ben, blinking, and I think his pupils might be getting smaller.

Thank God.

He turns to go.

"Don't leave camp," I add, hating how small and scared I sound. "Please."

He shoots me a glance over his shoulder. "Don't worry."

I don't want him to leave, but I have to talk to Julian. I need to know what they know about my fucking mom. "Just hurry."

Ben throws up a hand, an acknowledgment, and disappears into the night.

Julian's tent is empty.

I stand there for a moment, hoping they'll appear before me. Hoping I made some mistake, went into the wrong tent. But I didn't. And Julian is gone.

Then I see it: their walkie, discarded on the floor.

"Goddamn it, Jules." I bend to pick it up, but something's not right. It's *not* Julian's walkie. It's my mother's. But how...

The thought peters out and dissolves to nothing. I turn the walkie in my hand, and something catches my eye. Something I didn't notice before I discarded the thing under my bed. There's a triangular notch on the walkie's side, carved in the plastic, right at the seam. Curious, I dig my fingernail between the seams. There's a bit of resistance, and then the back half of the walkie loosens, coming away from the rest of the device.

I hold the two halves in my palms, their insides facing me, wires and battery pack, technological intestines. Did my mom make that notch? What am I looking for?

Then I see it — something against the inside of the walkie's back panel. Something I'm pretty sure shouldn't be there. I drop the other half of the radio; it clatters dully to the canvas floor. A torn piece of duct tape holds two objects against the back panel. One is bright pink and rectangular, garish in the night. The other is a metal half-sphere, with a pale, pulsing light at its center. I peel away the tape, taking the items in my fingers.

I immediately know what the half sphere is. One side of it is sticky, meant to adhere to any surface, but it's been out here for thirty-two years. The adhesive is weak. If it hadn't been taped to the walkie, it would have long since fallen free. I can't believe it's still working after all this time, that Ben's watch picked up on it. It's a locator beacon.

My mouth goes bone dry.

I hold up the other item, the pink rectangle, delicately between my fingers. It's a mini tape.

My heart races.

This was my mother's tape. She left it with the intention to be found.

For who? For me?

"Julian?" I say, tremulously. What, like *they* put this here? Like they're hiding under the bed, ready to jump out and declare that I'm on a prank show?

I sit on the cot, wracking my brain. I need a tablet, but only Ben has one. And he— wait. My watch.

I'm barely breathing as I slide the tape into the tiny hatch in my watch. The screen flickers and goes black. Then a vid starts to play. And I know immediately where this is. It's the forest. There's no sound; just grainy, dark footage of a writhing form. The vid is too small to identify who it is, but I know her.

It's Andrews.

And she's wrapped in vines, embraced from head to toe, suspended in the air between trees like she's being displayed. Crucified, worshiped, destroyed. The vines roil around her, and she shudders. Agony? Ecstasy?

The video gets blurry, like whoever's filming is moving fast. And then it's suddenly much closer. I see her face, even in the low-quality video on the tiny screen. Her eyes are closed, her head thrown back, her mouth wide open in what looks like orgasmic pleasure.

A single white flower blooms from her mouth.

The video jostles again, then cuts out.

There are a few seconds of staticky blackness, and then another recording begins. This time, it's the waterfall. The white flow of water looks like salt or snow.

The video cuts out.

That's all there is.

Fingers shaking almost uncontrollably, I eject the tape and shove it into one of my cargo pockets. I'm struck by something I can't deny. I feel it in my gut, in the flow of my blood, my very DNA: my mother left this tape for me. She left the walkie for me. She knew she would have a child just like her. And she somehow knew, even if she would have done everything in her power to stop her if she could, that her daughter would come back here one day.

Hurried and clumsy, I lace my boots. There's no time to grab a jacket, no time for a light. I know where I need to go next. The waterfall.

20

INTERVIEWER: And when you discovered she was missing, what did you do then?

VIRGINIA JONES: I went looking for her.

INTERVIEWER: You knew being alone could pose a danger, but you went anyway.

VIRGINIA JONES: I had no other choice. I couldn't leave her out there.

INTERVIEWER: Your report states that she was alive when you found her.

VIRGINIA JONES: Yes.

INTERVIEWER: But you know as well as I, Ms. Jones, that she never survived the encounter in the forest. There are those who believe you killed her. What do you say to that?

VIRGINIA JONES: I wrote a report. I documented everything.

INTERVIEWER: That report isn't available to the public. What would you say to the friends and families of those we lost on the Planet? The friends and family of Jennifer Andrews?

VIRGINIA JONES: I didn't kill her. I didn't kill anyone.

INTERVIEWER: But you know how it looks. One by one, your team members went missing. One by one, you found them... and watched them die.

VIRGINIA JONES (growing agitated): I tried to stop what happened to them. It's in the report. You weren't there.

INTERVIEWER: Early reports stated concern over a pathogen. A possible infection. But you reject that explanation as the cause of death. Why?

VIRGINIA JONES: Because that's not what happened to them.

INTERVIEWER: Did you kill them?

VIRGINIA JONES: I told you, I didn't.

INTERVIEWER: Then what did?

VIRGINIA JONES: Nothing.

INTERVIEWER: Can you elaborate, Ms. Jones?

VIRGINIA JONES: No one killed them. They were not murdered. They gave themselves over. They worshiped the womb of the Planet, one by one, and she took them.

21

THE NIGHT IS TOO KIND AS I enter the forest. Boughs bend to me; moss and ferns seem to follow my passage as I go deeper into shadow. If you're going to do it, I think, just get it over with. Envelop me in leaves and roots, grow a garden in my lungs until they burst, until my ribcage springs open, and all over me are flowers.

Just *do it then*.

But the forest only seems to want to watch me and touch me, nothing more. The spray of flowers that engulfed Ben's hand do not come for me. There is no torment of knotted vines to hold me captive, like Julian.

Because of that — or in spite of it — I'm enraged. I slam through the underbrush with a sense of vengeance, bitter and full of ire, hating these plants that want me and shun me, these green things that would consume my friends but not me. And my mother's walkie, the hidden tape lying untouched, waiting for me. What is it? A sign? A curse? A daughter's obligation?

Wherever the forest leads me, I almost don't want to

see it. I know I have to, that there's no avoiding it. I can't keep denying the fact that I came here for this. To answer the questions my mother never could. I always used to see a hole in the puzzle in her harrowed gaze, a missing piece. Before her death, even *she* didn't know what became of her team. Maybe she did, once, but over the years, she'd cut it all out, never to be recovered.

Maybe she'd hoped, despite herself, that I'd come and fill in the gaps.

I'm getting close to the waterfall. I can hear its distant roar. Just a few more minutes, and I'll be there. My boots fall heavy on dark soil, my fingers brushing lichen-crusted bark as I pass.

And when I finally reach it, the fall is just as I remember. Unbidden, lines from a poem unfurl in my memory, one my mother used to recite. I murmur it aloud. "Like a downward smoke, the slender stream..." I move toward the waterfall until I'm damp with it, "along the cliff to fall and pause and fall did seem."

I hook a hand on one of the mossy ledges, pulling myself up.

I follow the handholds alongside the waterfall, until they curve inward along the rock face, closer to the plunging water. And as I come up to the smoke-like falls, I see it: a dark space between the falling water and the outcropping, just large enough for someone to squeeze through.

"What did you put there?" I ask the night.

It's only a moment's work, a stretch of muscle and a grip of hands and fingers, before I'm ducking through the dark opening. My left arm and some of my hair get wet, but it's not as cold as I'd expected.

I find myself on my hands and knees in a damp cave. I fucked up not bringing a light with me. I press a button on my watch, and the screen glows white, just bright enough to see shapes against the darkness. My chest is tight with anticipation and dread. Something's here. Waiting for me.

I shuffle forward on my knees until I see something resolve before me: shapes on the ground.

My watch screen goes dark, and I'm plunged into blackness.

Holding my breath, as if the dark is toxic to inhale, I press the button. My watch lights up again, and I breathe in. I reach for the first item in the cave, a shapeless lump. My fingers close over soft fabric. Holding up my watch to the textile, I see that it's a jacket, similar to my team's utility uniform.

An unavoidable *knowing* clamors at my throat, threatening to choke me.

This is my mother's jacket.

I turn it over with one hand, the other angling my watch like a sad little flashlight. And there they are — her identifying initials: V.J. She left this here deliberately. She climbed up those moss-wet rocks, shimmied into this space, and laid out these items. For me.

Who else?

A heavy inevitability settles in my gut. I put on the jacket. I zip it up and button the collar at my chin. I prod my watch, so the screen stays on, and reach for the other shape in the dark.

My fingers touch something smooth and angular. A

box. I pry it open, and inside is a spiral notebook. I pull it out, glance at the front cover, and see that it's blank. On the first page, barely legible in the low light, a scribble of a name: Virginia Jones.

"Is this her fucking diary?" I breathe, the realization hitting me like a brick. Is this what I've been craving for so long? What everyone on Earth wished they had but could never get, no matter how far they pushed her in interviews? The most private thoughts of a woman whose world was ending?

My watch screen flickers out. I can't read this here; I have to get back to camp. I curse myself again for not bothering to bring a flashlight and shove the notebook into the pocket of my mother's jacket. Methodically, slowly, I begin to back out of the tiny cave, back into the open air.

I'm halfway down the mossy outcropping when I hear someone crashing through the forest.

Do I hear him? Or do I *feel* him approach? His boots on scattered leaves and loam, his hands brushing ferns, his shoulder passing close to a tree. My breath hitches as he pauses, leaning a palm on a tree trunk.

No, don't touch it. Don't let it come for you. I need you here, with me.

He keeps going, leaving the tree bereft.

As I drop to the ground and turn, I see him enter the glade. He looks haunted, like there's a world of weight on his shoulders. And when he sees me, it's like he believes, somehow, that I might lighten that weight. I would do anything to make that true.

It's then that I notice what he's carrying under his arm. A bundle of clothes. Our gazes meet.

"Where did you get those?" I ask.

His jaw tightens. "What the fuck are you doing out here alone again?"

I falter, taking a step toward him. "Are those Darcie's clothes?"

"It's too dangerous to be out alone."

"I should tell you the same! You went and looked for her, didn't you?"

He hesitates, looks away. Then he nods. "I had her location, Jones. I had to. Didn't think it would take long. I found these by the river. Her clothes, her walkie. All her stuff." He takes a breath, meeting my gaze again, and I hold it, knowing he needs whatever strength I can give him right now. Just like I need his. "She's gone," he continues. "Missing. There's no trace of her. I called for her for ages, searched all around, but I think... I think maybe she drowned."

Bile rises in my throat, and I swallow it down, painful and sour. *She didn't.* "We don't know that." It's a platitude, almost worse than if I'd stayed silent. But I don't know what else to say, how to comfort him, how to make this better when all I can see is the image of her under the water as I climaxed in the plain, of her sinking into the riverbed. Being swallowed up.

I choke on a dry sob.

"Come here," Ben murmurs, striding over to me. He wraps me in his strong arms. His gentleness feels wrong now, a sweetness just for me that I don't deserve. "It's okay," he says, his breath warming my neck. He kisses me there, burying his hand in my hair. I notice belatedly that he's dropped Darcie's clothes, letting them fall thoughtlessly to the forest floor.

I don't have to look to know that his pupils are dilated again. He's already intoxicated by the forest. I could stop him, before I, too, fall helpless to it. Darcie is gone. Julian is missing.

I *should* stop Ben.

But his mouth insists, pressing hungrily into my skin. His hands demand, pulling my hair and seeking lower. I'm not that strong. I, too, need comfort. I, too, need to be found.

I take his head in my hands and make him face me. He looks at me through heavy-lidded eyes, lips parted, soft, and malleable. Reverence radiates like heat from his body. I pull him in to kiss me and his eyes flutter closed.

His body may be reverent, but his mouth is sinful. As soon as I part my lips to deepen the kiss, he groans, hands at my hips, and slams me into him like he's afraid I'll disappear. His fingers dig grooves into my sides. I want him to kiss me until the forest grows over us and around us, absorbing and consuming.

He kneels before me, hands running down my sides, squeezing my ass, the backs of my thighs. His hands are burning. When he looks up at me, he's worshipful. He's overflowing with want. A feral glint flames in his darkened eyes.

"May I?" he asks, breathless.

I don't know what he wants, but I grant it. I'd give him anything. He can take me however he likes. Because I know he's mine.

I nod, and he groans a searing breath against my inner thigh.

Then, frantic, fumbling, he unzips my pants. Pulls them down just enough to gain purchase on my bare thighs, his thumbs digging in deep. I'm already wet for him, and I'm sure he knows it. He kisses me over my soaked panties and groans.

"Jones, you're unbelievable..."

The telltale ache builds in my core. The sight of him there, kneeling before me, his knees in the black soil, his rough hands on my tender skin, drives me to the edge. Desire nearly drowns me.

"Ben, *please.*" I don't even know what I'm begging for.

"Whatever you want," he says, "I'll give it to you."

Then he presses the lightest, faintest kiss to my core. I almost combust, right then and there. He hooks two fingers over my panties and slides them down so slowly I could die in the time it takes him to get them out of the way. It should be awkward; we should be giggling, tripping over our half-shed clothes in the forest, unable to remove our boots. Instead, this feels holy, exquisite in its imperfection.

I close my eyes and breathe deep, wanting this moment with Ben to last forever. The trees, I imagine, bend down to watch. The vines begin to uncoil, to hesitantly reach for us with leafy tendrils.

Ben finally kisses me, an almost chaste press of his lips to my aching cunt. An overwhelming pleasure rolls through me, and I have to bite my lip to near-bleeding to stop the orgasm.

Not yet. I want to draw this out as long as I can. I want to beg him for it.

He kisses me again, slower this time, his tongue flicking

out to taste me, and I sob at the perfect sensation. My hips jerk without my permission.

"Shh, be patient," Ben murmurs, his deep voice vibrating to my core. I roll my hips slowly as he devours me with mouth and tongue. He knows just when to apply pressure, when to pull away. It's like he can read my mind. Like we're one organism, a flawless creature built for pleasure and desire.

"Good girl," he rumbles. "I can feel you. You're close."

I moan, arching my back. Something soft and cool caresses my breast, tickling my nipple. Something else wraps around my waist, holding me upright. I gasp at the tender touches, my breath coming in shallow gasps. The ache grows heavy, heavy. I am coming undone. Ben's mouth is relentless, both gentle and violent.

"Look at me, Jones." He loves saying that.

But I almost don't want to. I almost want to come apart at the seams and join with the wind, I want to sink and *sink* into the soil like Darcie, forever drenched in the endless pleasure of the Planet. But Ben gave an order.

Eyelids fluttering, I look down.

My breath catches. Vines wrap around my torso, gentle, slowly snaking, titillating in their passage. Leaves brush my nipples. The forest has me in its lush embrace. I should be terrified. I should break free, take Ben, and run, back to the shuttle, back to our ship, away from this place forever.

But—

Ben gazes up at me from his place of worship. There's nothing but adoration in his eyes. He sees the vines and doesn't care. He's not afraid.

"There you are," he murmurs. "You were somewhere else. Stay with me."

And then he grips my thighs so hard I know he'll leave bruises. Holding me firmly in place, his tongue undoes me. I'm at the brink, fingers buried in his hair, sobbing with need, when he clamps down on my clit, sucking, holding pressure there, and I am finally free. Waves of perfect ecstasy roll through me, and I close my eyes.

A vine tendril slides down my belly, curling against me, delving, until it joins Ben's tongue between my thighs. The pressure is immense, the titillation a hundred times greater than in the plain. It's like I can feel myself from within and without — I am both the vine and my tight wet cunt; I am Ben's tongue, working me to oblivion.

I cry out, my orgasm crashing through me like a dark ocean wave. Like inevitability. Like the sweep of an infinite cosmos.

Waves of euphoria flow through me and finally ebb.

My eyes fly open, the aftershocks of my orgasm stifling and dying. My cheeks are wet with tears. I try to catch my breath, to look down at Ben, but something's holding me. Something's wrapped around my throat. My pleasure curdles to panic as I claw, frantic, at the cords across my neck. The vines that looped around my torso, squeezing my breasts, choking me so faintly it almost felt *good*.

"Ben?" I cry out, realizing he's been quiet. I no longer feel his mouth on me, or his tongue inside me. There are only vines and leaves. I gasp, a choked sob, wrenching the plants from inside me. They're wet with my cum, gleaming in the darkness. I fling them from me.

"Ben!" I shout again, my voice hoarse.

I rip the last of the vines from my body, violently, until I'm free.

But the fleeting relief dissipates the moment I look down at the form at my feet: A kneeling body, Ben's body. But it's only a shape, a form. He's no longer visible beneath the thick, undulating greenery. There are vines, flowers, a knot of green and vibrant growth where he should be. It's as if a small forest leapt up all around him. Squeezing him. Smothering him.

22

SAPLINGS SPROUT all around him and bend inward in a crown-like circle. Vines as thick as my forearms still move, tightening like pythons, around Ben. And as I watch in horror, flowers begin to sprout and bloom, opening too fast, too bright, too beautiful.

And worst of all, I'm taken by it. It is gorgeous, this undulating thing, this mass of life and verdant growth, the gift of the Planet. This hungry, desirous being.

Ben.

The vivid thought of him — his crooked smile, his arms around me, the way he sees me like no one else ever has — jolts me out of this rapturous reverie.

No, you fucking don't.

It's too easy for me to pull my boots free from the cacophony of growing things. To zip up my pants in a breathless, panicked rush. This place doesn't want me. It's Darcie, Julian, *Ben* it wants. Why not me? Or is it saving the best for last?

"Take me instead," I plead, grabbing the largest vine

and pulling with all the strength I possess. "Take me if you have to, but leave him the *fuck* alone."

I tear at the vines. I break one of the saplings in half, its delicate trunk split, dangling by a green strip of bark, its spindly branches crumpled on the ground. I dig my fingers into the mass of vines and tear, snap, and pull until I'm breathless and sobbing.

Let him be alive. Please, let him be alive.

You can't have him. Not now, not ever.

A ragged gasp comes from within me.

"Ben," I sob. I see him at last — brown hair, marred with plant matter. I crouch, wrenching leaves and vines away from him until he's free.

He's coughing, gasping. Still breathing.

I pull him away from the mess of vines and out of the circle of saplings, half laughing, half sobbing with relief. He stumbles and falls after me, landing roughly on his hands and knees. But he doesn't recover; he's still choking, pawing at his neck, pushing fingers into his mouth.

Something's caught in his throat.

"Let me," I order, and he meets my gaze with a disarming, terrible trust.

His body jerks, his brows drawn. He can't breathe.

I grab his hair in one hand and wrench his head back. "Open your mouth."

He does.

And before I can do anything, out from between his lips blooms a flower, white as the moons, sinister and hateful. Sickly beautiful. Like a goddamn *painting*. I crush it in my fist and pull, hard. There's a terrible resistance, and I wonder — is this it? Am I too weak to save him in the end? And then he cries out in pain, and I shudder, tugging with all my strength. Something breaks loose with a horrible squelching sound, and I fall back into the ferns.

Ben falls forward, retching something thick and bilious, metallic smelling in the night.

The flower hangs from my closed fist, its petals crushed to nothing, its roots hanging lank and dripping blood.

I throw the thing as far away as I can manage, into the dark of the forest, and scramble to my feet. I grab Ben by the armpits and yank upward. "We have to go," I say. "Get up."

He gets to his feet, unsteady. He's still coughing, half retching, but he's alive. He's breathing. He lets me drape one of his arms across my shoulders, and we stagger from that hateful glade.

Ben and I say nothing until we're safely within the perimeter of artificial lights, safe from the moons' caresses, the waving plain. We slump into the main tent, and Ben goes straight for the wine. He pours us each a generous glass and sets them on the table. Then he turns to me and takes my face in his hands. I feel small like this, helpless but protected, his cool touch soothing against my hot skin.

"Look at me," he says, and it's far different than the order he gave back in the forest, with his mouth between my legs.

I'm afraid to meet his gaze. Afraid that I'll see a depthless dark stare, that he's still lost to the vines and trees, that the Planet has claimed him for her own.

"Look at me, Jones."

I can't refuse him, and I feel a wash of relief when I see

that his eyes are back to normal. He's still mine. I saved him. For now.

"Are you all right?" he asks.

Of course I'm fucking not. "Fine."

"You're fine?"

I nod.

"I'm not fine, Jones." He pulls me into a rough, desperate kiss. I melt a little, letting him diffuse himself like this. Letting him unwind. When he pulls away, the tightness in his jaw has softened. "I'm not fine," he breathes. "What the fuck was that?"

He doesn't know how to articulate the horror of it, but I do. "It's what happened to Julian." *It's what happened to Andrews.* "There was a flower, blooming inside you. I had to pull it out." Terror glances through me, suddenly. "What if there's internal bleeding? We have to scan you—"

Ben shakes his head. "There's no internal bleeding. It was in my throat. That's all. I felt it."

"But your lungs, your stomach—"

"They're fine."

"But you're not."

He hugs me, kisses the top of my head. "I'm not."

We stand there for a few quiet moments, breathing each other in. I realize I'm still wearing my mother's jacket. My skin is prickling hot, my heart is still hammering in my chest. Julian and Darcie are still missing. Ben is only here because I was quick enough to save him. I am living my mother's nightmare, history repeating itself, and there's nothing I can do to stop it.

"Have a drink," Ben says, like he can see right through

to my growing helplessness and terror. "It'll settle your nerves. Then we make a plan."

A plan. What kind of plan could fix any of this? But he's in leader mode, ready to solve this with just a gun and bravado. If anyone can do it, it's a military man, right?

Numbly, I join him at the table, sipping my wine. It does feel good, the slow, thick warmth, drifting outward from my stomach to the tips of my fingers and toes. It does calm my nerves, just enough to think more clearly. But all I can do now is think of Andrews and Darcie, my mom's team all those years ago. The way the Planet drank them in, one by one.

I take a long, hard swig of wine.

Part of me believes I killed Darcie. That I was supposed to come here and do this, just like, I suspect, my mother was. To shepherd them toward death, one by one.

"I'm going to check on Fleming," Ben announces, standing.

"They're gone," I murmur.

He frowns. "Gone?"

"I went to their tent earlier, after— I mean, before we— when you were supposed to be getting me water. It was empty. They're gone."

"Fuck, Jones, when were you gonna tell me this?" He's angry now, but not with me. I wish he'd direct his ire toward the one who deserves it, grab me by the shoulders and shake me, demand answers. Demand the truth I'm finally beginning to know.

"There wasn't time," I protest weakly.

"Jill Jo-ones." The sing-song voice cuts through the night like an alarm bell.

I grab Ben's hand.

"Is that Fleming?" Ben says, turning toward the source.

A shape resolves just outside the tent entrance. A pair of glasses catch the lamplight, flashing once. "There you are, Jill Jones."

"There *you* are, Fleming," Ben says, standing to greet Julian. He drops my hand and moves toward the entrance. "You scared the shit out of us. You feeling any better?"

My first impulse is to go to Julian too, offer them some water, take their temperature. But something makes me hesitate. A warning in my gut. Julian hovers just inside the tent. Their hair is still matted with dirt and bits of grass, and — their eyes are still wrong. My chest tightens with fear.

Julian stares at me. "Well, well. I thought I might find you two together. How did Darce so poetically put it? Ah yes. Tweedle Ho and Tweedle Slut."

Ben makes a dismissive sound. "Whatever you say, now come on, let's get you something to eat."

"I'm not hungry," says Julian, not moving from where they hover, just inside the tent. Their gaze snaps to Ben. "Come with me instead, Ben. I saw the most wonderful thing. Come see."

"I'm not going anywhere," says Ben, taking a step toward Julian. "And neither is Jones."

Julian's gaze snaps to mine. Fear races through my veins. Their condition is worse than it was earlier — their tone is harsher, their gaze even more distant.

"Ah, I see," Julian says. "So you've decided to keep him for yourself."

I stare, confused. "What?"

Julian narrows their eyes, all their attention trained on me. "Ben. You think he's yours now, don't you."

"I don't..." I wrack my brain for context. What does Julian care if I hook up with Ben? They thought it was funny. They encouraged it. They joked about his push-ups. The two of them are *friends*, for God's sake.

"Fleming, come inside," Ben persists. "You just need some sleep. You're running a fever."

Julian takes one step toward Ben, but their eyes never leave mine.

"Ben," I say tremulously. "Come back. Away from Jules."

He turns back to me, questioning.

In that moment of distraction, Julian darts forward. Ben isn't expecting it. He barely reacts. The gun is out of the holster and in Julian's hands before anyone can speak, let alone stop them.

Fuck fuck fuck.

I should have told Ben about Darcie. About the tape my mom left. About Andrews. He thinks Julian has a fucking *fever*. I should have stopped him from approaching Julian. I should have, *should have*.

Ben holds up his hands, laughing a little. "Very funny, Flem. You got me. But it's not your turn with G-dawg."

"What's funny?" Julian says calmly. "Is this a joke?"

Icy fear grips my heart.

"Give me the gun," Ben orders. "Stop fucking around."

"I'm fucking around?" says Julian, their unnatural gaze darting between me and Ben. "Au contraire. I believe it was Jill who fucked around. In the forest. In the plains. In the forest... again?" They scoff. "And now it's time to find out."

Their hands are frighteningly steady, but at least the gun is pointing at the ground.

"Jules," I say softly. "I think you might be sick."

They turn on me, taking a step forward. Ben backs up, partially between me and Julian, his hands still in the air, appeasing.

"I'm feeling fine," Julian says. "Not sick at all. The question is, what the fuck is wrong with *you?*"

A chill runs up my spine. "I don't—"

"Yes, you do." They smile, a slow creeping curve of the lips. They raise their hands and point the gun at me. "You know exactly. First Darcie stopped Her from taking me, and now this. You're keeping him from us. You think you can have him forever? Ben belongs to the Planet, Jill. He belongs with *me.*"

I freeze in disbelief. Is Julian *jealous?*

"Put the gun down, *now*," Ben growls.

Julian completely ignores him. They won't let me go. Their hateful stare keeps me stranded, alone on an island where no one can save me. Maybe it would be better to let them fire a bullet through my heart. Maybe then I'd find peace.

"Everything the Planet sees, I see," Julian says as if in a trance, moving slowly toward me, gun trained on my chest. "She told me what happened to your mother. Give Ben to me, and it'll be easier."

"Put down the gun, and cut the bullshit," Ben demands. It's like he's in an action film, while Julian and I face off at the climax of a psychological horror. He thinks he'll reach them with reason and force. But they're too far gone now, and I think... so am I.

"Shoot me, then," I bait. "It doesn't matter if I'm dead. Ben doesn't want you. He'll never go with you, wherever the fuck you plan to take him. So get it over with and shoot me. See what happens."

Julian makes a sudden, jerking movement.

Ben lunges.

I throw myself sideways.

Pop!

Something slams into me, hard. A searing, white-hot pain explodes in my shoulder.

I crash to the floor, vision blacking out, my whole body clenched in agony.

Ben shouts my name over and over, and then there's a barrage of curses, a violent scuffle, and the crack of a fist against bone. If Julian fires that gun again, if they harm Ben, I will kill them. I'll take them down with me no matter how much it hurts. I'll carry them bodily into the forest and throw them to the ferns and vines. *If you even think of hurting Ben, I'll let Her have you.*

The pain in my shoulder threatens to overwhelm me.

"Jones," Ben says, suddenly close, suddenly right here. He takes me in his arms. "You're alive. Thank fuck, you're alive. I thought they — it's okay, baby. Show me where you're hit. Breathe. You're okay. Show me where they got you."

I try to open my eyes, then, but they're too heavy. My shoulder is an endless throbbing, a sharp and all-consuming agony. Ben's voice fades, growing further and further away, until finally, I'm drifting in the silent darkness, alone.

23

I WAKE up in my cot, aching and itchy with sweat. I jerk up upright remembering the gun, Julian, the pain —

"Nope," says Ben, coming to sit at the edge of my cot. "Lie down. Relax. You got shot, and then you fainted. I patched you up, but you're gonna need time to recover."

It all comes rushing back to me like a nightmare. Darcie, orgasmic, sinking into the riverbed. Julian, wild-eyed, accusing me, pointing a gun at me. And Ben. Kind, patient, oblivious Ben. What does he think is going on here? That we all have a regular run-of-the-mill fever?

"I see the wheels in your head turning," Ben says, stroking my hair. "But I need you to relax, okay? You're lucky to be alive. If you hadn't seen that shot coming..." he swallows, glances away. "Get some rest. I need to find Julian."

"But the gun—"

He pats his thigh, and a rush of relief crashes over me when I see the gun is there, safely holstered. "Fleming wasn't hard to disarm," says Ben, smiling in an almost self-

satisfied way. That alone, his sly bravado, sends a little thrill
to my core.

"Come here," I murmur, reaching for him, suddenly
euphoric with the realization that I survived being shot,
that Ben is still safe, that he's here, that his fear of my death
means he might care about me as much as I care about him.

"I gotta go."

"No, come here."

He hesitates. He's in my thrall, but his gaze is pure, Her
influence nowhere to be found. He'd do anything for me. I
see it in his face, this unconditional care. Every part of him
is focused on me right now. It hurts my chest.

He gives up resisting.

He crawls onto the cot with me. He knows exactly
what I want, and I love that. Straddling me, still fully
clothed, his expression trusting and already lit with undeniable desire, he pulls on my bottom lip with a gentle thumb.
His voice, when he speaks, is so deep, so tantalizing, so full
of carnal promise that I arch beneath him.

"If you had died," he murmurs, "I would have dropped
fifty nukes on this planet from space. There'd be nothing
left. Not a single growing thing."

I smile. I can't help it. I care about him, I realize, more
than I've cared about anything in my life. More than my
mother. More than this godforsaken planet.

"I'd do the same," I whisper.

He smiles back.

We're in a bubble here in my tent, a safe haven, and I
revel in the way Ben talks about my hypothetical death.
Like it would ruin him. Like he might love me. My gunshot
wound throbs, but the pain is distant, muted. All I care

about is Ben's weight on the cot with me, his finger on my mouth, the ache at my core. I wrap my hands around him and pull him down, our mouths tangling with needy moans.

He's so good to me. So good for me.

"God, you get me so hard," he rumbles between kisses, his hands seeking under my shirt, hot and rough against my skin.

Good.

"Undress me," I gasp, as his teeth find the tender spot beneath my ear.

He pauses, lifting himself up to meet my gaze. His hands brace on either side of me, his arms flexed. So gorgeous. "I need to be distracted, Ben. I need *you.*"

"You got shot." He nibbles my ear. "I could hurt you." He dips his head down, treating me to a long, deep kiss. He groans into me, and I respond, gripping his shoulders with ravenous fingers.

I realize with heady wonder that I hardly feel any pain, not with Ben's full weight on my body, not with his tongue in my mouth, not when I'm soaking wet and ready for him.

"It doesn't hurt when your hands are on me," I murmur. "Undress me."

This time, he obeys.

His movements are gentle but deliberate as he pulls my shirt up and over my head, careful not to jostle my bandage. He unzips my cargoes, removes them slowly, and sets them aside. I'm naked except for my panties, already almost completely undone. Every shift of Ben's muscles, his heated gaze when my bare breasts meet the night air... everything he does works me into a frenzy.

Delirious with desire, I run my hand from my breast to my inner thigh, sighing his name.

He's still fully dressed, gun still strapped to his thigh. He stands over me, his hot gaze roving over my form as if I'm a priceless artifact, a work of art.

"Look at you," he breathes.

I catch his gaze and with a distant spark of relief, see that he's still Ben, still mine. Not Hers. Never Hers. Not while I'm here.

Finally, he takes my ass in his warm hands. He squeezes once, then slides my panties down so slowly I could come from anticipation alone. When he starts to shed his own clothing, I reach up, grabbing his wrist.

"No," I say, breathless. "Keep them on. Unzip your pants."

He does as I ask, his gaze never straying from mine.

"Take out your cock."

He shimmies his briefs down, awkwardly, until his cock springs free. My mouth waters at the sight of it.

"Look at *you*," I can't help but echo his words. "You'll do anything for me. You'll give me anything. Would you fuck me just like this?"

He groans assent and falls upon me hungrily. His mouth takes mine with fervor, and I relish the uncomfortable pressure of his belt buckle jamming into my hip, the cold metal of his zipper pressing on my belly. There's something perfect about him just like this, like he's a soldier designed just for my pleasure. All I need is his exquisite cock.

But I still want more. I want everything. And whatever I am, whatever I have to give, it's his. Forever.

I close my eyes as he kisses my neck, his mouth moving to my collarbone, my breasts. I gasp, arching my back as he sucks on one nipple, then another. He bites, gently. And all the while, his bare cock slides against my pussy, up and down, building that friction I need so badly. I'm soaking wet. If he angles himself just so, he could slide in... he could fill me up, slamming into me over and over.

I'm so close already. All he'd have to do is apply the right pressure in just the right way. My skin is on fire. I grab at him, almost delirious, kissing him, rubbing against him desperately, needing more.

"Ben," I gasp.

He understands what I want.

Inhale: he draws back, the tip of his cock teasing at my entrance.

Exhale: he slams into me so hard and deep that I slide up the cot, its frame shuddering.

I cry out a muffled curse as he pulls out, then slams into me, again. Again. I've never felt anything like this. With only a few thrusts I'm already on the edge, ready to fall.

For a moment, it's as if the tent is gone. The cot is gone. Nothing exists but Ben and me, our bodies moving together in perfect tandem, taut with pleasure. He, fully clothed. Me, naked and dripping with sweat. My wound is open and bleeding, red dripping from the bandage. But it feels beautiful to me.

"I need to touch you," Ben murmurs, stilted, like he's so close to coming it takes everything not to.

I let him pull out of me, as bereft as it makes me feel. I let him grab me by the hips and flip me over. My eyes flutter shut as he pulls me up to lean against him, my back against his chest, head against his shoulder. He lifts me by the hips, just enough — *fuck* — and slams into me again from this new, deeper angle. A moment later, his hands slide around to my front, one teasing my nipple, one dipping low to tease my cunt with purposeful fingers.

This is Heaven. This is bliss. And when his fingers curl upward, applying pressure to my clit as he fucks me, I sob with ecstasy.

"There," he growls, his breath hot against my ear. "You like that?"

His belt buckle jingles with every thrust. His dog tags stick to the sweat on my back. I'm vividly aware of the gun, strapped to his leg. With that thought, my core tightens, and a wave of orgasmic euphoria consumes me.

Julian leans against the tree, head bowed, hand braced against silver bark. They're breathing hard, but shallow. Their other hand dips below their waistline, moving steadily. They fall into the tree, their shoulder braced against the trunk, their face a mask of pleasure. Their head falls sideways, and their cheek presses gently against the bark.

"You're so close," Ben murmurs. "You feel so tight, so wet, so perfect. I could fuck you for days, Jones."

The ache inside me tightens and tightens until I'm gasping, writhing under Ben's touch.

Gnarled boughs lower themselves slowly. The twin moons light the plain all around, the grass shimmering, reaching as always, reaching eagerly toward Julian.

Ben stops thrusting. He holds me, his fingers pressed to my sensitive core, as wave after wave of pleasure rocks through me.

The tree at Julian's back begins to morph. Its bark moves and curves to open up, revealing a horrible blackness beyond. Julian sighs, throwing their head back, sinking into the dark as if it's thick black oil. And the tree nudges them in, its roots curling around their feet and ankles, pulling them down, down into the maw.

I begin to descend from my climax at the same time that Ben comes, and I'm almost swept up again as he gasps my name, making helpless little sounds as he empties into me.

As we descend from that impossible high, I return to myself one molecule at a time, slowly sinking down from the heavens. The sky fades and dims, and we are back in the tent, and it's just me and Ben, body to body, this quiet connection.

He lays me down gently, mopping my brow. He tucks me in with tender words. He zips himself up. He gently cleans my wound, and I barely notice. I'm still delirious with pleasure, even as the pain returns. I'm wrung out. When he replaces my bandage with a fresh one, I can hardly keep my eyes open. He murmurs more low-pitched words, reassuring, and intimately soft. And when he's satisfied I'm comfortable, he disappears for a moment. Soon, he returns with a cup of water and a cup of pills, and I swallow both, too exhausted to protest.

I'm on the verge of unconsciousness, unable to let myself drift off, terrified that when I wake, Ben will be gone.

I can't think about Julian. I won't. It was a nightmare. Unreal. Just like Darcie. None of this can possibly be real.

"Jones," Ben says, my name an endearment. He kisses

my forehead. "I need to go find Fleming, okay? Dose them up with something strong. Your painkillers will kick in soon. Try to get some sleep."

But it's not the pain I'm worried about. It's Ben, out there. With Her. It's Julian. It's Darcie. "Stay," I protest, my voice far away. My eyelids are so heavy. I'm so tired. "Stay with me."

"I won't be long."

"She'll take you..."

"Shh. Go to sleep. I'll be back before you know it."

———

I wake up in the dark, my shoulder an aching pulse. My head aches, too, and my body is sore, stiff, resistant to movement.

I roll over to my uninjured side in the cot, peering into the dark as my eyes adjust. "Ben?"

No answer.

I check my watch, and it's three o'clock in the morning. My heart sinks. Ben's gone. Everything in the tent, our fucking, his sweet words in the aftermath, is a blurry haze. Either I'm losing my grip, or those painkillers were *strong*. Sitting up gingerly, I flick on my lantern, blinking in the sudden light.

And then it really sinks in: Ben went after Julian. *Jesus*. He'll never find them. Julian's gone. And I left my walkie in the plain, discarded with my jacket.

I have to go get him, bring him back here. He could be wandering in the plain, the forest, all alone. I can't just sit here fucking around, gunshot wound or not.

Gritting my teeth against the pain, I lean over the edge of my cot, reaching for my clothes, and something catches my eye. My mother's jacket. It's draped across a chair that Ben must have brought in, now ruined with my blood. And discarded on the floor, probably after falling out of the pocket while Ben was tending to my injury: my mother's journal.

I sit there, motionless, watching the notebook as if it will make a sudden movement, or disappear.

Go find Ben. Go get him before something happens to him, if it hasn't already.

The journal calls to me.

I slide out of bed slowly. My shoulder burns. I get on my hands and knees, and a strange sensation pulls my gaze down. The floor is carpeted in plant growth. A shiver curls through me. Was it always like this? Did it grow just for me? Digging my fingers into the moss, I know it was the latter. I fucking *hate* it. I'm about to rip up clods of the growing things, pluck them from their beds, and crush them in my fists when something stops me.

A voice.

No, a sensation, a knowing. It's the same thing I felt when I pressed bare skin to the trees in the forest and knew their ages. The same call I felt when I discovered my mother's waterfall for the first time. The horrible desire for decay, to sink in, to be swallowed whole and cradled in Her womb. The same way I always feel Ben when he moves through the forest.

I listen intently.

The grasses whisper beneath the twin moons, flowing like a sea, undisturbed. Until... There — Ben. I feel his movements, boots against dark soil, body pushing through tall grass. He's alive.

Thank God.

I reach for my mother's journal, pulling it into an embrace. Then I crawl back into bed, gasping as my shoulder jostles, the notebook in my arms. I'm breathing hard; even that small amount of movement has winded me. There's no way I can go after Ben now. I'll just pass out on the way.

And this journal is important. I need to read it now, to understand this place. To understand my mother, to understand *myself*. She left it for me, knowing that I'd come here. And whatever truth she left in these pages? I can't go on until I know it.

24

From the Journal of Virginia Jones

Day One

I CRIED when I first saw the Planet. Just a green-blue speck in our viewscreen. So much like Earth, but so different. This planet is new and perfect, fresh; ready for humanity. And we won't fuck it up this time.

Day Two

The Planet herself is beyond articulation. She's beautiful. Gorgeous. I'm assuming if anyone reads this, they're from Earth. But just in case: Earth, humanity's home planet, is dead. We still live there but by the skin of our teeth. It's scientifically and biologically improbable that we've survived there so far past our expiration date. Hydroponics and genetically modified greenhouse crops, solar energy, over-processed nutrient "food", and a species-wide stub-born optimism have kept us going.

But our time is almost up.

So here we are, finally knocking at the door of a potential new home. And she's the most perfect, lovely thing I've ever seen. Six others are with me, exploring this miracle planet, to see if she's viable. To see if she could be humanity's new home. I have high hopes.

Day Three

Not sure how to describe this... *damn*. It's just that my thoughts move faster than this shitty pen. Okay. We went out in groups to "survey the perimeter", as John put it. He and two others are military, generally pointless but good for organization/efficiency.

For some reason it makes me feel better knowing someone has a gun.

The strangest thing: there are hardly any animals here. We knew it going in, the probes had indicated as much, but... to see it is bizarre. There are some small rabbit-like things, deer-like mammals, and waterfowl, I think I saw, flying in the distance over the river. The wildlife is almost recognizable? Similar to Earth's, which gives me the creeps.

The zoologist, Andrews, doesn't seem as perturbed. "Well, it makes sense if the conditions were similar to Earth," and so on. No, it doesn't, and she knows it. There are no insects. No apex predators. Just lots of plants and help-less, edible animals. What evolutionary model explains *that*?

Oh, get this! I buried the lede. When we went to survey

the perimeter, per John's instruction, wherever we went, the flora sort of... followed. It tracked our movements! Reacted to touch! It was like... God, how do I say this? The plants here behave almost like they can sense us, beyond just touch. Like they're curious about us.

Sounds insane, I know. But the flora here seems *sentient*.

Day Three, Night

Writing this down before I fall back asleep, so I don't forget. I dreamed the flowers and trees and things were coming into my tent. Then I woke up in a thicket, and I couldn't move. It was terrifying. Claustrophobic. A nightmare. But then I heard this voice, like it was soothing me from the inside out, like the trees and flowers were suddenly talking to me. Caressing me. And I wasn't scared anymore.

Day Five

We've been here for days, and I'm beginning to feel like I'm in a simulation. Every time we run a test, it comes back perfectly in favor of human life. We tested the groundwater, and it was perfect. The air is perfect.

If I was a religious person, I might have truly believed God made this planet just for us.

Until today.

Andrews and I were exploring the forest, looking for who the fuck knows what. Something to write home about beyond, "Wow, this planet is unbelievably ideal in every way." We came across these trees that were so ethereal, I was really struck by them. So, we hung around and inspected them, bagged some leaf and bark samples. It took us a while. Part of me wanted to just stay there forever, underneath those quiet branches.

We actually sat there for a while in the moss and ended up falling asleep.

When we woke up, it was obvious we'd been asleep for hours. And our feet were covered in growth. Little vines twisted through my bootlaces. Flowers bloomed at my knees. It was so thick we couldn't move. It took us ages to free ourselves, and we couldn't use our knives for fear of injuring each other.

Andrews thought it was fascinating, beautiful. She wanted to bring everything back to study. I made her leave it.

I'm still shaking as I write this. I can't get it out of my head.

What if we hadn't woken up?

Day Five, Night

Just got back from a midnight walk. I was wound up after that thing with the plants growing over us, figured I needed some fresh air and perspective. Maybe it's just a harmless mechanism of the native flora and nothing at all to be afraid of.

But I never got a chance to think about that. The voice from the other night came back. It sounds silly, but the voice was *velvety*, almost. It wrapped around me and held me. I felt safe. It felt like one of those dreams where you immediately trust someone, or love someone, even though they're a figment of your imagination.

I don't think this was a figment.

It felt real. And — I know it sounds impossible. But I was out there in the plain, alone. No one else around me. And this voice, this entity or whatever it was, it took my hand. I *felt* it. It kissed my neck.

And I'll never forget what it whispered in my ear:

You're finally home, Virginia Jones.

Day Seven

Everyone's pissing me off. They're hovering like little nursemaids. John insisted on taking my temperature, which turned out to be normal. Obviously. I'm not sick. I'm just tired, anxious.

From my perspective, none of my behavior has been erratic in the least.

Day Ten

The entity came to me again. I've been waiting for it. For *Her*. Everywhere I go, I feel Her watching. When I touch the grass, it's Her I'm touching. When I lie on my back in the moss, under shady trees, she cradles me against her chest.

It's funny — I haven't changed my mind about the Planet. It's that I understand Her now. She's not *just* a planet. She's so much more than that.

Day Thirteen

Andrews and I argued. I don't even know what about. She said I'm "not present anymore," which means nothing. I'm right here, aren't I? Just because I like going on walks alone. Just because I'm not going to her tent as often anymore. I don't have time for a relationship, let alone one with pointless conflict. Especially not here.

So, I cut things off. It was just a workplace fling anyway.

Day Fourteen

Andrews is gone.

I don't know how. I don't understand. She was in the forest. She radioed me. I went to look for her, and... well, she's gone now.

I can't get the image out of my head. It happened near this waterfall, where we went together once, alone. It reminded me of this poem that Andrews liked too. Tennyson, maybe. *To fall and pause and fall did seem.* I don't remember the name of the poem.

Part of me wonders — is it my fault? I broke up with her, and now...

But *She* helps me. She comforts me, tells me there's nothing I could have done. She was there with me when Andrews was taken. Her arms were around me.

And at night, She... it's crazy to write this. But no one will read it, not for a long time. At night, She comes to me, and we make love. She's there with me, in my bed. She touches me and caresses me until I come. But I can never quite see Her. She's like smoke or fog. There, but... not.

Are we fucking? *Am* I insane?

The saddest part is that I

Day Thirteen, Night

I didn't finish that last one. John went missing while I was writing. All his stuff is here. Even his boots. If he wandered off, he did it naked.

So now we're in lockdown. Nobody goes anywhere alone. They handed out guns to everyone, even us scientists, which seems unwise. I won't fire mine. There's nothing to shoot but each other.

Day Sixteen

She comes to me every night. She caresses me, touches me, kisses me until I'm molten. She's the one thing that's good in this fucked up nightmare. One by one, they're disappearing. And now I know what it means.

I know where they're going.

I shouldn't write this, but *someone* needs to know.

It's not safe here. We aren't safe here. It's a planet-sized trap, a cattle farm, a breeding ground. It eats us. It eats us. It swallows us whole. Every night she comes to me, I see it happening, and I can't stop it, because I

It's not my fault. It's not my fault. It's not my fault. It's not my fault.

Day Seventeen, Night

Only two of us are left. I don't know what to say. If anyone from Earth finds this, they'll know what I did. ~~That I gave myself to Her and let Her feast on them. I didn't warn them. I let it happen.~~ I'm certain our deaths are coming. I smell it in the air. The Planet hasn't had Her fill yet.

Day Eighteen

I took a test. I was sick this morning, and I had this awful feeling. Intuition? Instinct? I don't know. I don't know. It came back positive. I'm pregnant, which is impossible. I haven't touched a dick in my life. I don't even *like* men. It was a false positive. Had to be. So the last pair of us, Devi and I, took a scan. And there it was. An embryo, growing inside me. Brand new. Devi thinks I fucked someone and won't admit it — John, probably, the only good-looking guy on the expedition. I wish I had. But other than Andrews, the only thing I've fucked is Her.

Day Nineteen

I'm alone.

We were doomed from the start; I'm not an idiot. I can draw conclusions, just like any other scientist. It's all played out the same way each time. At first, I had hoped it was a correlation. Just strange, horrible visions. Now I'm certain it's causation. The things I see in my head when I come, when I'm with Her... they *are* real. And not just that. I'm killing them.

Andrews. John. Devi, all of them.

They were taken. Absorbed into an infinite womb. The belly of a planet. ~~I guess they're not *dead* in the way that we~~ I would have been next.

Instead, I made sure I was the one who got to lie for Her. I promised Her one thing: If she let me go, I would give her everything she wants and more. She's hungry, ravenous, all the time. But she won't have me. I'll give her something better. I'll be Her emissary to Earth. I'll bring Her everything she could ever want. I'll fill her up by the millions if She's patient.

But She won't touch me again.

Me, or my daughter.

———

Listen to me. If you find this, if you're here...

I hope to God you're not, but I have a horrible feeling you won't resist her call. She's part of you. And that's my fault, and I'm so sorry. But do me a favor, okay sweetheart? Don't let her take you. You're stronger than that. You have to be. She's your mother, but so am I. And if I raised you, I know you'll be a stubborn bitch.

I love you. I'm sorry.

25

SUNRISE. I've been reading for hours. Shaking, I set the journal aside. Relentless pain throbs in my shoulder. My thoughts clamor, none of them taking hold for longer than a few seconds. I need more pills. Ben hasn't come back. I'm cold. I pull the covers up. My mother—

My mother.

I force myself to finish the thought: My mother made a deal with the Planet to save herself and me. *Me*, already growing in her womb.

I don't want to think about this now. I can't think about it. The thought of Ben comes to the fore, and with it a heavy fear. He's still gone, and I need to find him.

The early morning light makes the tent glow pink-pale, and I know the dawn will be sweet and mild, like every dawn on the Planet, and I hate it. Maybe it's a bad sign, maybe I'm on the verge of a breakdown, but I feel strangely calm. Detached. In shock?

I take a deep breath, my lungs expanding and filling with cool morning air.

I drag myself out of the cot, and notice a cup of water and three pills on the bedside table. I take them, drink the water. Between the pain in my shoulder and stiffness from the cold, it takes a while for me to lace up my boots, but I manage it. Then I pull on my mother's bloodstained jacket, biting back a hiss of pain as I do. I leave the journal where it is.

Ben is my priority.

As I step out into the morning, I pause, listening. I know Ben went looking for Julian, and the last time I heard him, he was in the plain. He'll eventually find Julian's things by the tree they used for target practice. That hungry fucking tree. On this insatiable fucking planet.

I close my eyes. I feel the grasses in the plain drifting like waves, the wind caressing their silver-green blades like a lover. But I don't feel Ben.

Fuck.

I kneel, pressing my palms to the earth, turning my attention to the forest. I feel dew-heavy ferns, ancient trees, even the rush of the waterfall. But I don't feel Ben.

Cold fear slices through me, more painful than my wounded shoulder. He's gone. She took him.

I take off at a dead run.

The plain sighs, whispering sweet nothings as I charge through its hateful grasses. I crash through a spray of bright blooms, and I grab them in my fist, yanking as I pass. I *hate* this place. This horrible, too-perfect, miracle place. We were never meant to be here. We should have stayed away. But how could we, when it was built just for us?

How many others, I wonder, my chest burning with exertion. How many other lifeforms have come here, to a planet designed for them, and been *swallowed whole?* Entire civilizations? Or was the Planet ours, all along, and she simply lay in wait for billions of years, hungry?

I don't think so. She's lush, robust. Full of energy. She is well fed.

My mother's team, Darcie and Julian — they were just snacks.

And in the distance, I can make out the tree, stark against the verdant sea of the plain. Maybe I'm not too late. Maybe there's still time to save him.

I'm already winded, my boots catching in the dirt, the grass clutching at me and slowing my progress. The grasses pull at me, relentless. And the wind blows against me, stinging my face, slowing me down. The tree never seems to get closer. An entire planet, working against me.

Who the hell do I think I am? Injured, exhausted, running full tilt toward the black pit of fate. My whole life, I've been no one. Nothing. The shadow of my mother's worst memory. I should just stop. I should lie down right here and sleep until She takes me. She, who is so much more, and so much better than me.

My gait slows. I choke on saliva, trying to catch my breath.

The grass clings to me, strokes me. Maybe I'm exactly where I'm meant to be, closing the circle. The rustle of wind through the plain seems to agree. I could never save Ben.

But I'll miss him so much.

You just have to be Jones. You're more than enough.

His words come to me unbidden, a lifeline, and I cling to them. I think of his smile, the way he held me, and kissed my head, his touches so tender and so true. He is funny and real and kind, and so vividly alive. And he cares about me. Maybe even as much as I care about him. Ben sees something that I never had before. Something even my mother didn't.

He sees *me*.

And there in the plain, my energy flagging, my heart threatening to break, I grasp onto the one thing that feels right. The one thing I can trust, the thing that makes me feel like I'm worth something:

Ben. My beacon, my anchor.

I grit my teeth and keep going.

The tree rises up before me. It's impossibly perfect, a symmetrical statue against the sky, God-like in its form. She designed it for us, a beautiful tree to admire, to entice us. To make us let our guard down. The shallow clear waters of the oxbow-shaped river. The stillness of the dark, cool forest. The waterfall. All of it. Constructed just for us.

I can't help the shiver that runs through me at the sight. The tree is dark, its bark swirled with silver grey. Thick gnarled roots curl into the soil, its branches reaching upward at perfect angles, pleasing in their composition. I can't help but feel a sort of awe at the way the leaves fan out above me. The way the sky hangs purple above me. The grasses waving at my feet. This arresting feeling, this deep inspiration, the tightening waves of an orgasm — they are all a sort of worship, aren't they? She asks for this before She takes us. Feed me, love me, know me.

"Ben," I whisper and come back to myself.

There is Julian's pack, nestled in the roots of the tree. A knot forms in my throat. This is where I saw them last, sinking into the trunk itself, the gaping maw. I feel the urge to retch, but something about the quiet tableau calms my stomach. I should be terrified, disgusted.

But it is *so beautiful*.

I walk slowly around the tree, the slam of my heart in my chest a million miles away. Drawing closer, I reach out my hand, clambering over the massive roots until my palm is flat against the trunk. Life pulses through the tree, vibrant, gorgeous life. The Planet may be a perfect construction just for us, a simulacrum of the evolutionary process, but it *is* alive. It's *real*.

"Can you hear me?" I breathe.

A breeze picks up, lifting tendrils of my hair, caressing my neck and ears.

I can hear you, She says, not in so many words. But I understand Her.

Something crunches under my foot. I bend to pick it up. Ben's walkie. My chest clenches. He wouldn't have left it here, not without purpose. I imagine him wrenching it from his jacket as the tree pulled him into its womb, hot and throbbing. Maybe he was calling for me. Maybe he was pissed, fighting. Maybe he didn't know what was happening until it was too late.

I stare at the device in my hand like it's the alien thing, so different from the tree, the Planet, the seed that gave me life.

"What do you want from me?" I whisper.

She doesn't whisper back.

I drop the walkie, and it clatters against the roots. Ben was here. Ben, whose mouth on mine was everything.

Whose touch was more perfect, more real, than any tree or waterfall.

In a rush, everything comes into focus. My throat burns. I hear distant screaming, and a moment later realize it's my own voice.

No, no, no.

"Ben!" I cry hoarsely, pressing my ear to the tree. As if I'll hear him inside, calling for me.

Nothing.

But the wind, laughingly, almost smug against my skin, confirms he's there, just beyond reach. Just like the others, he was swallowed up.

I slam my fists to the trunk, over and over, raking them down the rough bark until I'm bleeding. Blood from my hands drips down to my elbow.

"Give him back to me," I beg, my throat raw. "*Give him back.*"

But she doesn't reply.

This can't be it. This can't be how I lose him.

I sob brokenly and press my forehead to the bloody bark. *No.* I was not put in my mother's womb just to relive her worst trauma. She knew that I'd come back here, but she also believed in me. I can do more than just this. Ben saw it too: I'm Jill Jones. And I'm a stubborn bitch.

The wind picks up, the grass undulating like waves all around the island of this tree. This fucking bitch. This celestial monster thinks she can have whatever she wants. But there's one thing she won't have, and it's Ben.

"Give him back to me," I say, ice-cold.

The tree remains motionless, impenetrable.

I won't give up that easily. I'm the daughter of a planet.

I'm Gaia, given form. I have power, too. Power enough to save him.

"You can't fucking ignore me forever, bitch." The words fall molten from my mouth. "Give him back to me."

Why should I? The wind seems to say, laughing, swirling around me, picking up my hair and tossing it over my eyes.

I turn to face the plain, bracing myself against the tree. "Because I'm your daughter. I understand you. And I know what you want, because..." I remember Ben's hands on my skin, his tongue and fingers and cock inside me. I remember the forest coiling around me as I came. I remember the ecstasy beyond anything I'd ever felt before, the rising plea-sure and indescribable crash of climax. The *worship*. The admission feels like a purge, a horrible truth: "Because I want the same thing."

Ahh, says the wind. *And?*

I could leave this place right now, just like my mother did. I could declare the Planet non-viable, a danger to humanity, and off-limits. The ECE would listen to me. It would be the second time an entire team has gone missing, and at that point, the circumstances won't be ignored. Maybe the world will accuse me of murder, just like so many did my mother. Or maybe I'll walk away scot-free, left to live whatever life I have left in peace.

But I know deep down that if I leave now, I'll never escape Her. She's part of me. She'll poison me from within, haunting my dreams. And She'll bring me back, helpless to resist Her call.

I could stay here then, allowing myself to be taken, just like them. I could become one with the Planet. Part of me swells at the thought, knowing that I'm ready. I'm a woman, but I'm also *Her*. The beating heart of everything living here, an unending hunger, desire; the crash of waves upon a shore. It would be so easy to stay.

Or I could do what my mother did. I could save the one thing I give a real shit about, the one soul I would do anything to keep. And for that, I can make a bargain.

"Listen to me, you cunt," I grit out.

The wind whips at me, pulling on my mother's jacket. Tree boughs bend in the gale, leaves fluttering away into the wind. Clouds gather above in a sudden storm, black and white-edged. She's angry. Trying to put me in my place. I won't let her.

"Give Ben back to me, *unharmed*," I shout above the wind. "And you'll get what you want."

For the first time since we arrived here, rain begins to fall. Heavy, pelting drops. They sting my skin with cold, and I'm forced to crouch, gripping the tree roots to keep myself from blowing away in the gale. She'd rather drown me than grant this one fucking thing.

"Give him back to me," I scream, drowned out by the downpour. "Give him back to me, and you can have them. *All* of them. We'll go back to Earth, we'll tell the ECE you're viable."

I'm drenched to the bone, hair plastered to my face. My mother's jacket flaps around me as if it's trying to drag me into the storm. I shrug it off, and it flies up into the sky, disappearing against the black clouds. The pain in my shoulder is gone. I feel nothing but desperate power sloughing off me as I scream at Her. The rain steams as it hits my skin. I could crack a fissure in the ground so wide it breaks the Planet in half. But not even that would stop her. Only this can.

"There are billions of people on Earth," I yell up at the roiling sky. "They'll come here. They'll colonize. If you're patient, as years pass, they'll build cities. We have the technology, the infrastructure, to bring millions here. We'll make you our new home."

My throat hurts from screaming into the gale. The pain in my shoulder returns, and I gasp, clutching at it with freezing-wet hands.

"Let Ben go," I murmur, my words swallowed by the wind, "and I promise you'll be fed."

26

THE RAIN STOPS. The wind dies so suddenly I nearly stumble and fall. Within seconds, the black clouds dwindle and clear, and the sky is once again a bright cerulean. A few soft white clouds remain. It's as if the storm never was, a violent argument diffused with a single sentence.

I push drenched hair out of my face, shaking. My hands are swollen and seeping, red with blood. I've bled through my bandage and my shirt. I turn to face the tree. It's unchanged, unblemished. Fear blooms in my belly, but I try to quell it with quiet words.

"My mother is the reason I'm here," I sob, half-choking on tears and phlegm. "She kept her word, didn't she? And so will I."

She's listening now. I feel Her contemplating. This is all I have.

"Let him go."

And then, just there in the wood — a crack begins to form.

Breathless, I watch as it grows longer, wider. My heart

threatens to burst in anticipation. The fissure opens, but there's only blackness within. I claw at the edges of the opening until the blood on my fingers stains the tree.

"Ben," I plead. "Ben, come back."

The fissure widens.

A shoulder appears. I recognize Ben's jacket emerging from the darkness, illuminated in the pale morning light. I grab him and pull, screaming as my shoulder flares in pain at the exertion. The crevice expands. Ben's head finally comes into view, brown hair matted and wet, like he's been digested and made whole again, slick with the insides of this godawful tree.

I pull and pull, tugging with every last vestige of strength left within me. I'm starting to think I'll never do it, that She freed him just enough to taunt me, to show me how weak I am. How human I am. That I was right all along: I'm nothing.

But I won't give up.

I'm sure I'm about to pass out from the agony and effort when I finally wrench him free. I fall back, dragging him bodily from the maw. As soon as his booted feet fall from the dark fissure, it closes behind him. The bark knits itself together until there's no hint that an opening was there at all.

I lie there, breathless among the tree roots, for I don't know how long. I realize, finally, that Ben isn't moving. Dread tightens in my throat. He's just unconscious. After all this, She wouldn't give me a corpse. Would She? I drag myself up to my knees, heart thudding. If She killed him...

I clamber awkwardly to Ben's side, heart in my throat. I check his pulse with blood-encrusted fingers. And when I feel the telltale throb at his neck, I sob brokenly. He's alive. Barely, but he's alive. He's here. He's still mine.

"Ben," I whisper, kissing his temple, gently touching his hair, pressing my forehead to his. "You're okay. I saved you. Wake up."

His eyelids flutter.

I hold my breath. My entire world hangs in the balance.

Then he opens one eye and immediately scowls, blinking. "Where am I?"

Tears stream down my face. I throw myself over him, kissing his face and neck. He smells like earthworms and ancient soil. I've never smelled anything better.

"With me," I sob. "You're safe. I made sure you're safe. She won't take you again."

After a few minutes, when we're both able, I help him sit up. He's strong and recovering quickly. He's *safe*. And I hate that I'm grateful to Her for giving him back to me like this, returning him whole. I guess she knows I won't keep my end of the bargain otherwise.

Ben rubs an unsteady hand over his face, then looks at me.

Really *looks* at me.

Dappled sunshine softens his expression, leaf-made shadows dancing across his eyes. And somehow, something in his gaze makes me feel like he's seeing me for the very first time.

Maybe he is.

Maybe he sees my mother's daughter, grown from the seed of a planet.

I can't help but wonder if he also sees, in the stricken

darkness of my gaze, what will happen next.

We won't stay here. The mission is complete. We'll go back to the shuttle, back to our ship, which orbits the Planet. We'll chart a course for Earth, and on the way, I'll put together a statement for the Earth Colonization Effort: Julian and Darcie are dead. I'll say it was a slow-acting post-hypersleep ailment or a simple fever. I'll say we honored their last wishes and buried them here, on the Planet. No one will question it; no one will look into it too deeply. And if their families protest, the ECE will pay them off. The ECE will be too focused on the fact that the Planet passed all our tests. They'll see in my report that we ran every possible experiment, each one a success. The ECE won't need much data to convince them. They'll acknowledge there are no remaining options for humanity, and that will be that.

I won't go back on my word. She'll know if I do; She's part of me. She always has been. I refuse to lose myself to her. I refuse to put Ben at risk.

So, I'll support the ECE when they officially declare the Planet viable and ready for human colonization.

Within a year, colonization efforts will commence. By that time, maybe Ben will have questioned me. Or maybe he'll still be glad to have made it, to be one of only two left standing.

I imagine all the years that will pass, the money and manpower spent to ready humanity for the journey across the stars, right back here, to the Planet. It will take trillions of dollars and several years. And by the time we set out on the long adventure, millions will have died on Earth — from weather events, illness, starvation, or worse.

But that won't happen to us. Ben and I will be treated as heroes, kept safe from whatever ails the rest of the world. We'll be asked to join in the colonization effort. We'll be paid a ridiculous salary. And if I know the ECE, we'll be offered a spot on the first ship.

We'll refuse.

And one day, I can't guess exactly when — but one day, Ben will outright ask me why I did this. He'll ask me why I wrote that report. He'll ask me why I lied about Julian and Darcie's deaths, why I signed off on the Planet, why I lied and sent millions out there without any warning.

Maybe I'll tell him. Maybe I won't. Maybe, by then, he'll have figured it out.

I do know one thing: As long as he stays far away from Her, he'll be safe. Even if he grows to hate me, even if he sees a monster where a woman used to be, it won't matter. It will be a weeping wound in my heart for the rest of my pathetic life, but it will have been worth it.

It will have been worth it because he'll be safe.

And when colonists begin to die, when they're taken away, one by one... at least it won't be him. *At least it won't be him*. Even if he hates me, it won't be him. Even if he wants me dead, it won't be him.

Ben lifts a hand, pressing a thumb against my chin. I realize I'm crying. He brushes my tears away, sweet and gentle. Almost reverent. Almost worshipful.

"Jones," he breathes: a benediction. As if he sees me for everything I am. As if he understands me. As if I'm *everything*.

Maybe, I dare to hope, turning my face into his touch... maybe, when that day comes, he'll forgive me.

ACKNOWLEDGMENTS

As always, thank you to Rachel Wharton of Page & Proof, who is not only the best editor in the world but also one of my best friends. I continue to have no understanding of commas, what they are, or how to use them, and Rachel always sets me right. My books would not be what they are without her.

Thank you to my beta readers, Lords of Writing (Rowan, Maggie, and Katherine), you understand my unhinged concepts like no one else. To my hype readers and blurbers, I would not have had the balls to publish this book without your support. Logan, De, Callie, Lyndall, Rose, Taylor, Nikki, Brooke, Becca, Lindsay (and anyone else who I forgot to write in my notes app list), you are so important to me! Thank you/I love you.

Special thanks to my early readers, my champions, my heroes. Every graphic, review, reel, post, whatever it may be — helped make this book happen. And, more importantly, you got people to preorder it. Magnificent work!

And thank you of course to *Stargate SG-1*, particularly a brief yet intense hyperfixation on Lt. Colonel Cameron Mitchell.

Finally, Adam, my darling husband, your support and love saved me from countless writing-related breakdowns. Thank you so much for existing! I owe you my life!

ABOUT THE AUTHOR

Meg Smitherman writes romantic stories about magic, kissing, and horror in space. Based in Los Angeles, she shares her life with a chihuahua, a cat, and a handsome Englishman. When not writing, she keeps busy playing video games, curating Medieval music playlists, and planning tattoos she'll probably never get.

If you love Meg's books, please don't forget to leave a review!

And if you want to keep up with Meg's upcoming releases and sneak peeks, subscribe to her newsletter: https://authormeg.substack.com/

Follow Meg on social media:
    Instagram: @megsmitherman
    TikTok: @megsmitherman

ALSO BY MEG SMITHERMAN